Thursday Trials

*Also by Colleen L. Reece
in Large Print:*

Alpine Meadows Nurse
Belated Follower
Come Home, Nurse Jenny
Everlasting Melody
The Heritage of Nurse O'Hara
In Search of Twilight
Nurse Julie's Sacrifice
Yellowstone Park Nurse
Mysterious Monday
Trouble on Tuesday
Wednesday Witness

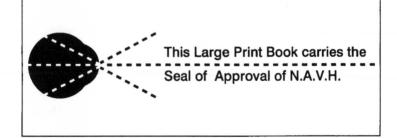

This Large Print Book carries the
Seal of Approval of N.A.V.H.

Thursday Trials

Colleen L. Reece

Thorndike Press • Waterville, M·

Published in 2001 by arrangement with Colleen L. Reece.

Thorndike Press Large Print Christian Mystery Series.

The tree indicium is a trademark of Thorndike Press.

The text of this Large Print edition is unabridged.
Other aspects of the book may vary from the original edition.

Set in 16 pt. Plantin by Elena Picard.

Printed in the United States on permanent paper.

Library of Congress Cataloging-in-Publication Data

Reece, Colleen L.
    Thursday trials / Colleen L. Reece.
        p. cm. — (Juli Scott, super sleuth ; bk 4)
    Summary: Sixteen-year-old Juli hopes her experience
as a trial witness in a bank robbery case in Bellingham Bay,
Washington, will give her material for writing mystery
stories, until she and her church group friends receive
death threats and warnings not to testify.
    ISBN 0-7862-3201-3 (lg. print : hc : alk. paper)
    1. Large type books. [1. Robbers and outlaws — Fiction.
2. Christian life — Fiction. 3. Writing — Fiction.
4. Washington (State) 5. Mystery and detective stories.
6. Large type books.] I. Title.
PZ7.R2458 Th 2001
  [Fic]—dc21
                                      00-054469

Thursday Trials

Chapter 1

Sixteen-year-old Juli Scott dashed into the blue and white kitchen of her Bellingham, Washington home, waving a piece of paper like a banner. Her blondish-brown ponytail bounced and her glowing blue eyes shone like twin sapphires. "Mom, Dad, guess what!"

Gary Scott, Juli's police officer father, leaped from his chair. His white teeth flashed in a wide smile and the corners of his gray eyes crinkled. "A magazine accepted your Christmas story? Congratulations!"

Juli made a face. "I wish! Would you believe I haven't even written it yet? Anyway, it's less than six months until Christmas, too late to even be considered for this year."

Anne Scott, an older replica of her daughter, stopped washing lettuce and smiled at Juli. "There's always next year," she encouraged. "So what's the big news? Did Shannon win another writing contest?"

Sidetracked for a moment, Juli laughed. "No. She's still gloating over the $750

7

second prize she won for her magazine story 'Katie.' She's also started a return-to-Ireland fund — and she wants to take me, too." Juli fell into a reasonable imitation of her Irish-born friend's brogue: "Mercy me, we'll be for goin' someday."

Her parents chuckled, but Dad reminded, "You haven't told us your news. Since you've ruled out all possibilities of a manuscript sale, may I remind my one and only daughter that Mom and I are waiting to hear what's on that piece of paper?"

Juli grinned and did some secret gloating of her own. All possibilities of a manuscript sale had *not* been ruled out, although neither Dad nor Mom knew it. After several rejections, Dad had grown discouraged about the mystery story he wrote while on leave from his Washington State Patrol job. But Juli hadn't. She believed any story Hillcrest High's honors writing teacher, Mrs. Sorenson (AKA Allison Terrence, author), pronounced good deserved publication.

After the last rejection and Dad's announcement he wasn't going to try again, Juli stepped in. She secretly sent "Murder in Black and White" out on her own. Now she crossed her fingers, hoping it wouldn't do another "homing pigeon act" as Dad called it.

8

"Well, are you going to tell us, or aren't you?" Dad said, a little impatiently.

Juli came back to Earth and the Scott kitchen. "I am." She turned the paper over. Before she could continue, a *rat-a-tat-tat* on the front door was followed by an excited call and the sound of racing feet.

"Hi, everyone." Juli's best friend Shannon Riley burst into the kitchen, much as Juli had a few minutes earlier. Her blue-gray eyes, accentuated by incredibly thick lashes the same crow-black as the bangs above them, looked enormous. She stared at the paper in Juli's hand and held out an identical page. "You got one, too. I knew you would."

"One what?" Gary Scott pretended to tear his thick, dark hair. "We've been trying for the last ten minutes to find out what Juli's holding."

"That's right, second daughter." Mom smiled warmly. "A special invitation?"

Shannon's laugh rang in the summer-warm kitchen like the chime of a silver bell. "You might say so." She laughed so hard tears came.

"A verrrry special invitation," Juli said with a roll of her r's. "We've been subpoenaed. Isn't it exciting?" She grabbed Shannon and waltzed her around the kitchen. "Just

9

imagine! What better way for me to see justice at work than to be an actual witness at a trial? It will give me firsthand experience so when I write my young adult mysteries, I'll know exactly what it's like." She stopped so suddenly Shannon nearly fell. "A writer can only learn so much from TV trials."

Her father snorted. "Don't expect the fireworks and carrying-on you see in TV trials," he warned. "The real thing is a far cry from TV movie theatrics."

Shannon dropped into a chair and said in a small voice, "Do I have to go?"

"You mean you don't want to?" Juli knew her astonishment showed in her voice. "It's the chance of a lifetime."

Her friend shook her head and looked glum. "For you, not for me." She hesitated, then brightened. "Hey, I know. I'll plead the fifth."

Caught in a daydream of herself helping bring a criminal to justice, namely, one Brett Jones, accused of several local bank robberies, Juli absentmindedly echoed, "The fifth?"

"You know. The Fifth Amendment. All I have to say is, 'I refuse to answer on grounds it might eliminate me.' " She smirked.

After the same stunned silence that always greeted Shannon's misquotings and

10

mispronunciations (these had long since earned the label "Rileyisms" at school, church, and among friends), the three Scotts roared.

Shannon put her hands on her hips. "What?"

"It's *incriminate,* not eliminate," Juli choked out between giggles.

Shannon's chin went into the air. "So? I'll be so scared the judge will have to eliminate *me* after the first question. Besides, I don't know anything. Neither do you, right? How come we got subpoenaed?"

Gary Scott grew serious. "Simply because you girls and several others of the church youth group ended up at the Pizza Palace at the same time someone, probably Brett Jones, robbed the Chuckanut Community Bank across the parking lot the two businesses share."

Juli's keen mind seized on a single word. "Why do you say probably? He confessed, didn't he?"

Dad laughed. "Yes. Force of habit, I guess. Besides, until he is actually convicted, Brett is the alleged thief. Anyone who has the remotest knowledge of the case is considered a witness. I imagine the others in your group have also been summoned to appear."

"That's right," Shannon put in. She ticked the names off on her fingers. "Besides Juli and me, there are Ted and Amy Hilton, John Foster, Dave Gilmore, and Molly Bowen."

Juli's anticipation burst into words. "I hoped when we gave the police our statements we'd be called. Good thing Brett is insisting on his right to a jury trial. It's so cool!" She gave a little wiggle of pure excitement.

Dad told her, "That depends on your viewpoint. I'm sure Brett Jones isn't looking forward to what's ahead with anything except fear."

His reminder dampened Juli's enthusiasm. She twisted her fingers. How could she rejoice when someone, even a person who had gone terribly wrong, faced a long prison sentence? What must God think of her, selfishly viewing the upcoming trial as a research opportunity? Shame scorched her. *Sorry, God,* she silently prayed.

Juli remembered the way her heart skipped beats when Brett first came to church. Even though she really liked blond basketball player Dave Gilmore, Brett's dark eyes and flashing smile had attracted her. She and Shannon even nicknamed him TDSC: tall, dark, and super cool. They later

12

discovered he had lied about his age and had only attended church and school to check out Juli and her friends' identities. Yet it hurt to think Brett had not only robbed banks, he'd threatened each person he thought might have witnessed him at the Pizza Palace that fateful Wednesday. Juli shuddered, remembering.

That evening the rest of the crowd that so often hung out together gathered in the Scotts' spacious, tree-lined backyard for an impromptu barbecue. Sean Riley, Shannon's banker father, traded his business suit for a chef's apron and hat. He also tossed aside his crisp manner. He laughed and joked with the others while expertly tending the food on the barbecue.

"Mr. Riley, I'll bet it's a relief for you that the bank robber is in jail," Amy Hilton commented. The tiny blond cheerleader who claimed the spotlight whenever possible had been strangely subdued since Brett's capture. Juli and Shannon privately wondered if Amy had really liked him or was in shock from his arrest.

"I wish it were that easy, Amy." Sean's eyes, so like his daughter's, reflected troubled thoughts. "I may be a bit fey, as my Irish grandmother would say, but I have a

13

strange feeling everything isn't as finished as we may think."

"What does 'fey' mean?" someone asked.

"Visionary. Able to predict the future." Sean's laugh chased the gloom from his face. "Which I can't, of course. It's just a feeling." He smiled at the faces turned toward him. "Forget it, okay? Besides, the barbecue is ready."

An hour later, ten well-fed people lounged in deck chairs and on the grass. A light breeze whispered secrets among the gently waving flower stalks and leaves, shaking fragrance from a multitude of blossoms. It held a tang of salt from Bellingham Bay. Glistening stars peered down at the contented group. Juli felt her tension relax. It had been a long time since she'd felt so peaceful. She wanted to hold the time close and never let it go.

Before long, conversation turned to the trial which would begin soon. "I still don't see why we were called," Shannon complained.

"Why worry about it?" Dave Gilmore grinned at her from where he sat cross-legged on a blanket beside Juli. "We may not all have to testify. If we do, piece of cake. We're called to the witness stand for what? Maybe two minutes. We tell what we saw —"

14

"Which isn't much," Shannon put in.

Dave began again, as if he hadn't been interrupted. "We tell what we saw. Bingo. We're out of there." He stretched his long legs and leaned back on his hands. "What's so hard about that?"

"Nothing," Shannon had to admit. "Actually, that's what we saw. Nothing, except Brett's white Mustang in the parking lot. Naturally, none of us checked the license plate, so we couldn't even be sure it was his."

Amy took up the story. "Brett panicked because he thought we saw him. We didn't. Not even Ted." She looked at her twin, who resembled her, except he had brown hair and she had bleached hers blond.

"Right. I yelled at him but was too worried about Amy getting pizza on my letter jacket to even look up." Ted heaved a sigh and his blue eyes looked troubled. "I agree with Shannon. I'd just as soon not be called to testify."

"Of course you agree with Shannon," Dave teased. "She's your . . ."

Shannon jumped up before he could go on. Clear red showed in her smooth cheeks. "It's getting late and we need to clean up. On your feet, everyone."

"Yes, boss," Dave said. The others lazily

obeyed as well. In a short time, the dishwasher hummed. All traces of the barbecue had vanished except for the lingering aroma of spicy sauce.

"Thanks a lot," the guests told the Scotts.

"Anytime." Dad hospitably waved around the large yard. "We have the space, and since I took a desk job instead of being on patrol, I'm off most evenings."

"I'm celebrating that, plus being out of school for the summer," Mom quickly added. Her face shone with happiness at her husband's job decision. "I am also looking forward to only teaching half days in the fall. I'll have afternoons off." *And I'll be here when Juli gets home from school,* her steady gaze silently promised her daughter.

Juli wouldn't have cared all that much if Mom had actually said it. Coming home to an empty house for most of her sophomore year definitely hadn't been one of her top ten favorite things to do. The last part of the year, Dad had been there. Funny how much difference it made, even to a sixteen-year-old.

After everyone left and Juli's family shared a quick devotion, she crawled into a short cotton sleep shirt and curled up on the bed in her yellow-walled room. Comforters on the twin beds picked up the color, and

16

her cinnamon-brown plush teddy bear Clue patiently waited on her desk. His dark, shiny eyes and perky red plaid ribbon tied in a bow around his neck invited hugging. Juli grabbed him and the notebook she used for a journal, and began to write.

I really am sorry about Brett, Lord.

She stopped and nibbled the end of her pencil.

Dad and Mom always tell me I rush ahead of things. All I could think about was my big opportunity. You love Brett just as much as You do me, even though You hate all the terrible things he has done.

What made him the way he is? Why would any boy, no, young man, who obviously has a lot going for him, become a criminal? He's good-looking. He has to be smart, too, or he couldn't have carried off all the things he did for so long before getting caught. It's strange. What really proved Brett's downfall was his own guilty conscience. Otherwise, he wouldn't have been so suspicious, thinking everyone was against him.

Did You make him feel that way, God? Will he remember anything he heard about

You when he came to church or was with our youth group?

She paused and nibbled again. A burning question came to mind and she slowly wrote it down.

Lord, is Brett sorry at all? If so, is it for what he did, or just because he got caught?

Juli didn't know the answer to her question. She slowly put down her pencil, gave a sad little laugh, and hugged her teddy bear. "I may have a Clue, but I don't have an answer," she whispered to her furry friend. "No one knows but God, and He isn't telling." She yawned, put Clue back on her desk, and turned out the light.

While Juli wrote her innermost feelings in her journal, her friends dealt with their concerns in different ways. Dave Gilmore fell asleep almost immediately, firmly believing what he had told Shannon — their part in the trial would be small.

John Foster and his favorite girl, red-headed Molly Bowen, took it a little more seriously, but not much. As John said, "When you don't know anything, you can't testify to anything."

"I know." Molly agreed. She added, "I'll just be glad when it's over. Shannon is really dreading it." She wrinkled her freckled nose. "At least we'll all be there for her."

Sean Riley told his daughter much the same thing. "There's nothing to be afraid of," he quietly said. Yet the shadow in Shannon's eyes warned him even though she'd come a long way, she hadn't fully recovered from being abducted a few months earlier.

Amy Hilton lay sleepless, thinking about her twin's face when he said he wished he didn't have to appear in court. "It's because Brett took Ted to the hospital after he hit him," she mumbled. A quick trip to Ted's room confirmed it. Brother and sister agreed that if Brett were all bad, he would have simply let Ted lie there. They also agreed they could barely wait for the trial to be over.

Chapter 2

Juli, Shannon, and the rest of the youth group prayed the trial of Brett Jones would soon be over. They also talked a lot about it among themselves. Summer in northwest Washington State is a time to be outdoors. Gray skies turn electric blue. Fat white clouds lazily float by or pause as if observing the countless evergreen trees, blooming shrubs, and flowers. Bellingham Bay offers many places for walking on the beach and picnicking.

Whenever possible, the Rileys, Scotts, and any of the girls' friends who were available loaded into van, station wagon, or cars and headed out to enjoy. One evening after supper at Larrabee State Park, Juli, Shannon, their parents, Dave Gilmore, and Ted Hilton gathered in a circle close to the bay. White-lace-topped waves lapped against the shore. The mournful cry of seagulls wheeling in the fantastically colored sky of a dying day added a touch of sadness. The water of the bay shimmered rose and gold.

Juli broke the silence. "Being here in this peaceful place makes it hard to understand why people choose to do terrible things. It's so beautiful, it makes my throat ache." She felt herself blush and hoped everyone would think it came from sunburn, or was a reflection of the now-crimson sky. Putting her feelings into a journal only God and Clue saw was one thing. So was telling Shannon, or Dad and Mom. But blurting them out in front of a group was something else.

Dave shifted position on the blanket beside her. "I know what you mean." He sighed. "If Brett Jones had been what we thought he was, he might be here with us right now. It makes you feel weird, doesn't it? I wonder what's going to happen to him, anyway? Any jury will hand down a guilty verdict."

Shannon's Irish eyes looked enormous under her wind-tousled bangs. She looked across the circle at Gary Scott. "It's an open-and-closed case, isn't it?"

Dad smiled at the earnest girl. "I think you mean an open-and-shut case," he said kindly. A small frown darkened his gray eyes. "On the surface it appears so. On the other hand, who knows?" He shrugged. "If I've learned one thing in my years with law enforcement, it's this: You can't be a hundred percent sure of anything. No case is ever over —"

"Until the accused sings?" Shannon eagerly supplied. At the look of amazement on the faces around her, she quickly added, "You know. Like the man at the opera that told his squirmy son, it's never over until the fat lady sings."

The rest of the group roared. When Juli gained control, she gasped, "That has to be the worst Rileyism yet!"

"Or the best," Ted put in. "Shannon, you are absolutely priceless."

Not to be outdone, Sean Riley asked, "Speaking of priceless, when you were little, did any of your parents pay you to be good?"

"Dad!" Shannon looked shocked. "Of course not."

"What? Not one of you was ever paid to be good?"

"No," they chorused.

"I see." Sean's eyes twinkled until he looked more like Shannon than ever. "Then I'm to understand you were all good for nothing?" He threw up his hands in surrender at the howl of protest that rose. "Sorry. I couldn't resist."

"You didn't even try," Juli accused the tall man she had learned to love like a second father, but her laughing eyes softened her charge.

Sean grinned back at Juli, looking like a young boy caught with his hand in the cookie jar. "On to me, aren't you?" He stretched his legs straight out in front of him, leaned back on windbreaker-clad elbows, and gazed at the sky. "Look. The stars are starting to come out."

The others followed his lead. Millions of stars gradually brightened as the daylight faded. "Looking into the heavens always makes me feel small and insignificant," Anne Scott admitted in a hushed voice. She gave a low laugh. "I'm in good company. Thousands of years ago the psalmist David evidently felt the same way. He expressed it so clearly and beautifully." She clasped her hands around her knees and quoted, " 'When I consider thy heavens, the work of thy fingers, the moon and the stars, which thou hast ordained; What is man, that thou art mindful of him? and the son of man, that thou visitest him?' "

"Psalm 8:3 and 4," Dad said. "Don't forget the next two verses: 'For thou hast made him a little lower than the angels, and hast crowned him with glory and honour. Thou madest him to have dominion over the works of thy hands; thou hast put all things under his feet.' " He shifted position, put his arm around his wife, and added, "New translations of the Bible are helpful, but some passages need the majesty of the King James Version."

"This is definitely one of them," Juli agreed. She didn't add that hearing the solemn quotation in Mom or Dad's voice always brought little chills to her spine. It was another of those personal feelings best recorded in her journal, or whispered to God in her private prayers.

A feather touch of sadness brushed against Juli's spirit. When she was younger, she had shared everything with her parents. At sixteen, it was harder. Even though they had a great relationship, something inside her squizzled like plastic wrap in a campfire when she thought of revealing her innermost fears and feelings to others. Even someone close.

It must all be part of growing up, she knew, of maturing from girl to young woman. Most of the time she found it exciting. Yet now and then, in poignant moments like this, Juli wished she could go back to a more carefree time. Or at least fiercely hold onto the present. A little prayer winged its way to heaven. *Please God, help me be what You want me to be, and thanks for always being there for me when I need You.*

A chuckle splintered the fragile moment. "Are you asleep?" Dave Gilmore wanted to know. "Or just pretending to be in a trance so you'll get out of helping clean up and pack our stuff?"

Juli scrambled to her feet. "Sorry." She helped him fold blankets and collect trash so they'd leave the park as tidy as when they came. "I guess I just don't want tonight to end."

"I hear you clear and loud, as Shannon would say," Dave agreed.

The Irish girl indignantly called, "I heard that."

"We know," Dave and Juli said together. They were rewarded by Shannon's laugh, like the chime of silver bells. No matter how many times her friends teased her because of her mispronunciations and misquotings, she brushed the jokes aside like dust from a mantel and joined in the fun.

That night when the girls crawled into the yellow-covered twin beds in the Scotts' yellow ranch-style house with its white shutters and brightly blooming window boxes, Juli said, "Know what?"

"What?" Shannon punched her pillow into a more comfortable shape.

"I wish I were more like you."

Shannon's Irish eyes went from blue to

gray. She sat bolt upright in bed, hair darker than ever above cherry-red pj's. The Irish brogue she seldom used came back as it always did when she was surprised. "Mercy me, why would ye be for wishin' such a thing?"

"Doesn't it ever bother you when we laugh at your Rileyisms?"

She flopped back on her pillows. "Not the weensyist, teensyist bit. Why should it? I know I'm for bein' loved." She thought for a minute and the brogue disappeared. "I suppose it might if I felt people were putting me away."

Juli tried not to laugh. She found it a lost cause. "I hope no one's putting you away! You mean putting you *down*. Putting you away is throwing you in jail or killing you."

This time the brogue was deliberate. It matched the twinkle in Shannon's eyes and the broad grin of her sensitive lips. "I'd not be for likin' that." The grin wilted and she turned on her side to face Juli better. "Can you keep a secret?"

Juli tried to keep hurt out of her voice. "You know I can." She suddenly had the feeling Shannon's mind and spirit had left the bedroom and taken flight to faraway places. "What's the problem? Testifying in court?"

"Yes. I am so scared it makes my mouth dry when I even think about it." She ducked her head and stared at her tightly clasped hands. "My dad and the others know I'm scared, but no one except you knows how bad it is. What if I get up there on the stand and freeze? Or burst into tears?" Her face turned white.

Juli didn't know what to say. She slid from her bed and raced to her friend, wisely saying nothing. For a long time she just sat beside Shannon, patting her shoulder while Shannon spilled out all her fears. Shannon finally shook herself, managed a wobbly grin, and announced, "I think I feel better." A look of shock chased away the fear in her face. "Hey, Juli, I really *do* feel better. I guess I needed to tell you. Just having you know helps so much!"

"Good." Juli gave her a quick hug. "Is it safe for me to go back to my bed?"

Shannon giggled. "Yes, your super-sleuthness. Storm's over."

"There's no such word as super-sleuthness," Juli told her.

"There ought to be. You could put it to work and help me not be so scared."

Long after they turned out the lights, the wistfulness in her friend's voice made Juli twist and turn. Was there anything she

27

could do besides pray? She searched her brain but didn't come up with an idea. Sleep claimed her before she could use her "super-sleuthness" to solve the problem of Shannon's fear of testifying.

She awoke to another gorgeous day after a haunting dream. In the dream Shannon had been standing at the front of a courtroom calling, "Please, Juli, help me. You're the only one who knows." It made Juli more determined than ever to do what she could. If only she could ask Dad! He was bound to have encountered terrified witnesses during his career. Yet doing so would betray Shannon. The glimmer of an idea lit like a butterfly, fluttered, and grew. Excitement stirred in Juli. There was a way, but it had to be handled just right. She climbed into jeans and a pink top similar to the yellow one Shannon wore, and headed toward breakfast.

The pale green dining room waited, bright with dancing rainbows from the window sun-catchers and a multitude of blooming house plants. After the blessing, Juli fired the first gun in her campaign. "Dad, I'm the only one who's looking forward to testifying at Brett Jones's trial and that's because it will give me good background material for writing. Some of the kids are really dreading it." She avoided looking at Shannon. "What can a person do to get over fear?"

Gary put down his fork. "Have any of them actually visited a courtroom or seen a trial? Or are they basing their ideas on what they see on TV?"

"I've been in a courtroom but the rest of them probably haven't." Juli took a sip of orange juice. "Why?"

"It's easy to fear the unknown. What if I arrange for all of you who have been subpoenaed to observe at least part of a trial?"

"Could we just go in an empty courtroom first?" Shannon asked. Juli suspected her fingers were clenched beneath the sparkling white tablecloth.

Dad smiled across the table at her. He always took special care to be gentle with Shannon. "No problem, second daughter."

Her face shone like the White House Christmas tree. "Thanks."

"Think nothing of it." Gary Scott airily waved his hand. "When you have someone with connections, it makes sense to take advantage of him."

Shannon cut a piece of melon and ate it. "May I please ask another question?"

Dad laughed. "A dozen. A hundred. You should know by now this is the Scott Bed,

Breakfast, and Answer Emporium."

The laughter Juli expected didn't come. Instead, Shannon said in a low voice, "It's about Brett. Will he, I mean, can he get out on bail? Since he confessed and everything?"

"It's highly unlikely. The bottom line is, Brett Jones is a bad risk. He has no apparent ties to the community. There are multiple charges. Jones has been in trouble before. Any judge will set bail so high it's preposterous to think Brett can ever raise it." Dad grinned. "If you remember correctly, none of his successful bank robberies netted big bucks."

Obvious tension drained from Shannon. She slumped back in her chair.

"Are you worried what might happen if he does make bail?" Juli asked.

"I can't help remembering how wild Amy said Brett was that day at Mount Baker," Shannon slowly replied. "And how he came unglued when the police took him into custody and questioned him. He admitted everything."

"I know." Gary Scott glanced at his watch. "I have to go." He rumpled Juli and Shannon's hair, kissed Mom, and headed for the garage.

Mom sipped her herbal tea and smiled at

the girls. "I'm glad you didn't get summer jobs, except for your occasional baby-sitting in the neighborhood. It's nice having you both in and out." She stood, hugged each of them, and inquired, "What are you planning for today?"

"A bike ride this morning. The rest of our friends are tied up, so it's just us."

"Please, no running into Rottenweilers this time," Shannon teased.

"I don't make a habit of it," Juli haughtily told her. "You need to write on a chalkboard a hundred times, 'There's no rotten in Rottweiler.'"

"There is in some of them," Shannon insisted. "Besides, teacher, I don't have a chalkboard or chalk. I'll load the dishwasher instead. You can fix us a lunch."

"Shannon Riley, you are actually talking about lunch when you just ate four enormous pancakes and a whole lot of other stuff?" Juli demanded.

"Five, to keep up with you, but who's counting?" Shannon patted her flat stomach. "Remember the Boy Scout motto."

"Yeah. Be prepared." Juli picked up dishes and silver and headed through the wide arch to the blue and white kitchen. She loved the country-print curtains over the mini-blinds, and the blue-banded plates that matched perfectly. While Shannon loaded the dishwasher, Juli inspected the refrigerator's contents. "I'm so full nothing looks interesting."

Shannon relented. "We can pick up something later, if you like." She peeked in the cookie jar. "Mmm. Chocolate chip. Okay to take some with us?"

"Sure." Juli handed her a plastic bag. "Mom, we'll bake more this afternoon." A sudden thought struck her. "Hey, want to go bike riding with us?"

The sudden pleasure in Anne Scott's face showed how much she appreciated being asked, but she shook her brownish-blond head. "Wish I could. I promised to take one of the women from church shopping. Another time, maybe." Her warm smile thanked them. "Have a great time."

"We will," they promised. Ten minutes later, the riders started out, but not in the direction where the dog Shannon called a Rottenweiler lived.

Chapter 3

Nothing on Juli and Shannon's bicycle ride through quiet, tree-lined streets and up and down hills was unusual. Nothing happened to spoil the day. No witnessed crimes. No Rottweilers rushing at them. No knowing homework waited when they got home. Just the simple joy of being out of school and together in perfect weather.

For several glorious, carefree hours the girls alternated between pedaling and resting. They stopped for snacks when breakfast became only a fond memory. "Today is another page in our diary of life," Juli poetically announced.

"I love being with the rest of the group, especially Ted," Shannon replied. She stretched out on freshly mown grass in a park on their way home. A lovely pink colored her face. "It's also nice when it's just us."

Juli's tongue took a swipe at her melting ice cream cone. "We don't have to be anyone except who we are."

"Are we ever?" Shannon giggled and yawned. She looked dappled where sunlight stole through leafy maple branches above her and played tag on her upturned face.

Juli pointed west toward Bellingham Bay in the distance. "We'd better make the most of today. Clouds are gathering like fans at a ball game." She watched the great silver-tipped masses churn and boil into gigantic, fantastic shapes. "They're starting to move fast." She stood and brushed her jeans. "We have to get a move on, too, if we're going to outrun the storm."

"I suppose so." Shannon sounded re-signed. She got up and shook tiny blades of grass from her clothes. "Wonder if we'll make it. Those clouds look like they just held a convention and decided to attack the earth!"

"Right." Juli mounted her bike seat and took the lead. By the time they reached the Rileys' two-story brick home with its carved front door, the sky wept great drops that spattered in the dusty street and created a pungent odor. "Made it!" Shannon panted as she and Juli sprinted to the safety of the porch.

"If we'd gone the few blocks on to my place, we wouldn't have," Juli gasped. The last mile had been on level ground, but they rode it at top speed. The girls sat down on porch chairs as a lightning flash lit the sky, followed by a loud peal of thunder. "How far away is the center of the storm?" Juli wondered aloud.

"I've heard you can tell by counting 'one thousand one, one thousand two,' and so on between the flash and the thunder crash," Shannon said. "Each 'one thousand' is supposed to be how many miles away the storm is."

Sizzle. Bang! Crash! The thunder came so close after the next flash it shook the many-paned windows of the Rileys' house — there was no time to count. "It must be right on top of us!" Juli shouted. Another boom drowned out her voice. For a good fifteen minutes the storm raged before moving on to flash and rumble in the distance. A half hour later, the beating rain stopped. An apologetic sun slunk out from behind the vanishing storm clouds and beamed down on the drenched earth. Small birds twittered. Robins caroled. What few clouds remained harmlessly drifted against the freshly washed, cobalt blue sky.

"That was really something." Shannon pulled her knees up to her chest and wrapped her arms around them. "Good thing the rain came. As dry as it's been, that lightning might have set dozens of forest fires."

"Yeah." Juli stared from the retreating storm clouds to the small, innocent white ones. "When you were growing up in Ireland, did you watch clouds and see pictures in them?"

"For sure." A look of remembrance came into Shannon's Irish face, along with a touch of mischief. She made her voice deep and mysterious. "Some people are for sayin' Irish clouds come in the form of leprechauns, shamrocks, and the Blarney Stone."

Juli snorted. "You sound like you kissed the Blarney Stone once too often!"

"I do blather on a bit, especially when it comes to talking about the Emerald Isle," Shannon admitted. She didn't sound a bit sorry. "Wait 'til I take you there. You'll come home raving as well."

Juli dropped her teasing. "Do you really think we'll go someday?"

"God willing," Shannon told her, still under the spell of childhood memories. "I do love clouds, don't you? Even ones without leprechauns and —"

"Enough, enough." Juli tilted back in her chair until the legs squeaked in protest. "Mom had a golden oldies radio station on the other day. You know, one that plays songs from the 50s and 60s, sometimes the 70s. Anyway, there was this cool song that talked about looking at clouds."

"Did it talk about recalling illusions? I think it's called 'Both Sides Now.' "

"Yes. It says the singer really doesn't know clouds, or love, or life at all." Juli took a deep breath. "That's the way I feel sometimes." She glanced quickly at Shannon to see if she understood.

The look in her friend's face and quick nod showed she did. So did the way she reached over and patted Juli's shoulder. "When I start thinking that way, I remind myself I'm only sixteen," Shannon softly said. "God doesn't expect us to have all the answers."

A rush of love for her faithful friend brought mist to Juli's eyes. "Thanks."

"For what?" Shannon asked, but her smile showed she didn't expect a reply. A moment later she bounded up from her chair. "You better call Mom, now that the electrical storm is over and it's safe to use the phone. If she got home from shopping, she'll be wondering where her lost daughters are."

"Let's just go home," Juli suggested. "We can be there practically as soon as we can call. Leave your bike and I'll walk mine."

It didn't take long to reach the Scotts'. By the time Mom got home, a pan full of chocolate chip cookies sent an inviting aroma from the oven. The timer buzzed. Juli stuffed her hand in a padded kitchen glove and took out the pan just as the phone rang. "Mom, can you get it? My hands are full." Half of her attention on the cookies, she cocked one ear to see if the call was for her.

Seconds later Mom called, "Turn on the TV. Quick."

"I'll do it." Shannon raced to the living room.

The pan of cookies clattered to the stovetop and Juli ran after her. She almost collided with Mom in the doorway. Shannon stood frozen in front of the TV. "What on earth . . . *that's Dad!*"

Juli and Anne Scott pushed up beside her and stared at the picture. Tall and imposing as ever, Sean Riley stood between two city police officers in front of the bank where he worked. A half-dozen squad cars, several other uniformed officers, and some unidentified people crowded the background. Not a trace remained of the laughing man who had joked with the happy group less than twenty-four hours earlier.

One of the officers opened the door of a

squad car. A grim-faced Sean crawled inside. A quick turn onto the street, and the car disappeared.

Shannon gasped. Her eyes grew enormous. "What are they doing with Dad?"

For one horrible moment, doubt crept into Juli's heart. The next, she felt scorched with shame. "They're not *arresting* him," she said. "He got into the front seat, not the back."

Shannon's knees buckled. She caught the edge of a chair and broke her fall. "I — I don't understand."

"Shhh." Mom reached for the volume control. A well-known Bellingham TV reporter stepped to the foreground and began to speak.

"We're live at the scene of a robbery," she stated. Excitement shone through her professionalism. "Minutes ago, yet another Bellingham bank was hit in broad daylight. It was thought that with the arrest of suspect Brett Jones, the string of such occurrences would stop. However, today's incident shows local banks are obviously still at risk.

"Bank personnel, including spokesperson Sean Riley, are cooperating with the police to the fullest extent and have been asked to refrain from comment until initial questioning has ended. We expect to receive an official statement later in this newscast. At this point, it is not clear whether today's episode is similar to or tied to previous robberies."

The reporter wrapped up her report, then the news anchorman added, "Stay tuned to this channel for the latest information concerning this breaking news, as well as other news, sports, and weather."

Juli perched on the arm of Shannon's chair and hugged her friend. "Your father is all right. Get it? He's all right."

"I know."

Shannon's dazed expression brought a rush of sympathy. How well Juli knew what she was feeling! The awful feeling in the pit of her stomach when she thought of someone she loved facing danger. The fear gradually giving way to relief. Thankfulness swelled inside Juli. Her own father's decision to take a desk job had brought more peace than she'd known in years.

A few hours that felt like an eternity limped by. Dad, Sean, and FBI agents Andrew and Mary Payne — who had been involved with earlier cases concerning the two families — arrived. Dave Gilmore and Ted Hilton were already there at Mom's invitation.

"Call the boys and invite them for

supper," she had whispered to Juli. "It will help get Shannon's mind off Sean." When they came, she turned over the entire meal preparation to the four of them. Juli sent her a glance of appreciation. Keeping busy was what Shannon needed, especially when reluctant newscasters had no further information about the robbery and could only speculate.

"Any leftovers for four starving people?" Dad wanted to know when they came inside. He sniffed and sent a mock glare at the cooks who swarmed into the hall from the kitchen. "Smells like spaghetti or lasagna. It isn't all gone, is it?" His joking manner didn't hide the concern in his keen gray eyes.

"We made enough for an army, and we haven't eaten," Dave Gilmore announced. "It's just now ready."

"Good thing. Andrew, Mary, and I would hate to arrest you on charges of obstructing justice by attempting to weaken the strength and morale of law officers," Dad grumbled. "You know where the bathrooms are, everyone. Wash up and we'll eat."

Mom and Shannon quickly removed china and silver from the dining room table, added another leaf, and reset it. Dave poured more water. Ted brought the enormous bowl of tossed salad and choice of dressings. Juli removed the huge pan of lasagna from the oven and put more garlic bread in to heat. "We can use the chocolate chip cookies for dessert," she muttered to herself.

Three seconds after Dad asked a blessing on the food, Juli looked across the table and asked, "May we talk about it now or do you want to eat first?"

Sean Riley sighed. "You're all so full of questions, you may get indigestion if we make you wait."

Juli started to agree, but a warning pinch of her arm from Dave stopped her. Juli looked at Sean's tired eyes, his deeply lined face. He looked exhausted. The last thing he needed right now was a rehash of the day. "I vote we take the chance," she said. She forced a laugh. "You know me. Once we get started, I'll get wound up and talk with my mouth full. It could be dangerous if I get excited!"

The look of gratitude in Sean's face more than repaid the disappointment of having to put off hearing his story. It also curbed Juli's impatience so much that after supper she told the five adults, "No KP duty for you. Go relax in the living room and get prepared for a thousand questions."

"Haven't I told you ten million times not to exaggerate?" Dave Gilmore asked, producing laughter that cleared the air.

Never had kitchen chores been performed so quickly. Soon Juli and her helpers marched into the living room with a large plate of fresh cookies.

Red-haired Andrew Payne barked, "Miss Scott, is this a bribe?" and reached for a cookie.

"Guilty as charged." She passed the plate to his attractive wife and the others.

Shannon sat down on the rug by Sean's chair. "Okay, Dad. What happened?" Some of the afternoon's strain still showed in her face. "When I saw you getting in that police car I didn't know what to think."

Her father chuckled. Now that he'd eaten, he looked more like himself. Juli was glad she hadn't insisted on discussing the robbery at supper. "All they wanted me for was to give their sketch artist information while it was fresh in my mind. Even a few hours can blur memories. I'll tell you one thing: If I'd ever considered a life of crime, that ride would have made me reconsider." He shook his head. "Funny. There I was, totally innocent, feeling like a criminal because I was in a police car!" He looked from the Paynes to Gary Scott. His blue-gray eyes twinkled.

"Maybe if you gave everyone a ride, it would cut down on the number of crimes and criminals."

When the laughter subsided, Sean told his story. "The robbery followed the pattern of the others in which Brett Jones took part, according to his confession."

"Which, by the way, may not stand up in court," Andrew Payne said sourly.

"What!" Ted Hilton's exclamation cracked like crystal dropped on cement.

Andrew and Mary exchanged knowing glances. "Jones has hired one of the shrewdest attorneys in Washington State. Ben Sharpe is notorious for finding loopholes and getting his clients off. The plea's been changed to not guilty."

"But Brett confessed!" Shannon protested. Juli shivered. The idea of Brett Jones running around free was not pleasant.

Mary explained, "Sharpe can always claim Jones was mentally disturbed, or emotionally unstable when questioned. Or that he was terrified, and the police intimidated him. He will make a big deal out of the fact the 'so-called confession' was made without the presence of an attorney, even though Jones was advised of his rights. He gave them up and babbled like a brook long before he ever asked for legal representation."

"Will a jury believe that garbage?" Dave sounded incredulous.

"It may." Andrew's face looked stormy. "I'd like to know where Jones got the money for his attorney. That guy doesn't come cheap." He tightly closed his lips and Juli wondered if there weren't a whole lot else he could say.

"Meanwhile, back at the robbery . . . ," Dave prompted.

"There was one big difference." Sean leaned forward in his chair and lowered his voice. "Instead of a lone thief, this time there were two persons. Similar height. Similar weight. Identical dress." He paused so long Juli's nerves silently screamed. "They worked together as if they'd been doing it for years."

Chapter 4

Heavy silence followed Sean Riley's announcement that two men instead of one had been involved in the robbery at his bank. Juli glanced from face to face. Andrew and Mary Payne wore the carefully guarded expressions Juli knew hid much and told nothing. Mom stared at Sean, apprehension in her blue eyes. Dad seemed intent on examining his fingers. Shannon, Dave, and Ted looked as if they'd been hit by a train. No wonder. The single difference in the most recent robbery's MO [*modus operandi*] could mean almost anything.

Juli found her voice. "Then it may be a copycat crime. Or two different people entirely." She laughed nervously. "At least we know Brett Jones isn't involved. He has an airtight alibi. You can't be sitting in jail and out robbing banks at the same time!"

Andrew Payne raised a red eyebrow. The corners of his mouth turned down. "Sorry, Juli. I hadn't gotten around to mentioning an important fact."

Her lips went dry. She licked them and

whispered, "You don't, you can't mean —"

"You guessed it. Someone posted bail. As of two o'clock this afternoon, Brett Jones walked out of jail a free man until his trial date." Andrew hesitated, then added significantly, "In plenty of time to be part of a robbery if it had been planned earlier."

"I thought bail was going to be so high Brett couldn't possibly raise it," Shannon protested. Her eyes looked more enormous than ever in her pale face.

"So did everyone else." Mary Payne reached over to pat Shannon's hand. She shot an inquiring look at her husband. At the slight shake of his head, she said, "It does make one wonder, doesn't it?"

Juli knew it was not what Mary had intended to say. She looked at Andrew's bland face, caught the warning in his eyes, and bit her tongue to keep from blurting out the suspicion forming like a hard knot in her stomach. *Item:* Brett Jones did not have the kind of money necessary to raise bail. *Item:* Neither could he hire a high-priced, unscrupulous attorney, as Andrew had described Ben Sharpe, on his own. *Conclusion:* Someone (or ones) a whole lot more important, a whole lot more powerful than one young man in his twenties had to be involved.

Her mind raced. When the Paynes first became involved in the Bellingham robberies, they had confidentially shared their orders: "Determine if the local robberies are part of the chain of thefts throughout the western states." Was organized crime behind them? Juli scoffed at the idea. People involved in organized crime wouldn't be messing around with robberies that took in only a few hundred dollars at the most.

But what if the incidents had been a test? A rite of initiation to help Brett gain entrance into an organized crime ring? Juli's spine tingled. She had seen ex-convicts on TV talk shows who served their time and straightened out their lives. According to them, it wasn't uncommon for new members to be asked to prove themselves. She wanted to spill out the startling idea but another glance from Andrew zipped her lips. Good grief, could the keen-eyed agent read her mind?

Evidently. When the talk session ended, Andrew cornered her in the hall, away from the others. "Do you ever play poker?" he asked.

Juli stared at him. "No. Why?"

"You should learn. It helps a person control his or her expression." His eyes bored into her like shiny steel drills. "There's a great deal at stake here, Juli, far more than just another bank robbery." He scowled and his laugh sounded more like a bark. "Ironic to refer to theft in such a way, but that's how it is." He paused, then added, "Mary and I have told those here tonight as much as you need to know, simply because you've been involved. You've also all proved you can keep your mouths shut."

His grudging compliment made Juli feel good, but Andrew wasn't through. "I hate to see a face as attractive as yours go deadpan. On the other hand, excitement such as you showed a little while ago can be disastrous if noticed by the wrong persons." He raked bony fingers through his red hair. "I don't know about the rest of your close friends. Watch it even around them. Got it?"

Juli felt her cheeks burn at the rebuke, quiet as it was. "Got it. I'm sorry." She glanced both ways, made sure no one was listening, and lowered her voice. "It's just that I wondered whether Brett's low-key robberies were an initiation stunt to get him accepted into the 'big time.' "

Admiration brought a shrewd grin to Andrew's lips. "Good girl. By the way, you deserve a reward for keeping quiet earlier." The likable grin that so changed him spread across his face. He started to say something more, but Shannon came into the hall, followed by her father and the others. Andrew ducked his head and quickly whispered in Juli's ear, so low she had to strain to hear it, "Ask your dad about the bail after the rest of us leave. I told him earlier."

The mystery in the agent's voice set Juli's nerves jangling. For once, she was glad Shannon wasn't staying overnight. The hint of promise in Andrew's words gave her hope that she might soon be able to make sense of Mary's earlier comment about Brett's bail. It took all of Juli's hospitality not to shove everyone out the door so she could ask her father what Andrew meant!

Juli somehow managed to control her growing bump of curiosity until she closed the door behind the last guest. Dad and Mom had gone back into the living room. She dashed in from the hall, dropped to the rug by Dad's chair, and said, "Come closer, will you please, Mom?"

Anne Scott deserted her seat on the sofa and plopped into a chair next to Dad's. Her blue eyes sparkled. "What's up?"

Juli pitched her voice just loud enough to be heard. "Andrew said to ask Dad about the bail." She hunched her jeans-clad knees and circled them with her arms. "What did he mean?"

Gary Scott grinned. "I might have known you'd catch that warning head shake Andrew gave Mary. It's just this. There's something mighty peculiar about the way the bail was posted. Authorities are investigating the source. They are *very* curious as to why anyone would be interested enough in Brett Jones to put up an enormous amount of bail. We already know he has no apparent ties to the community and is a terrible risk." Dad shrugged his shoulders. "So far, there doesn't appear to be a clear connection. I suppose that's why Andrew motioned for Mary not to say anything else tonight."

Juli scarcely dared breathe. "So that's what makes it peculiar?"

"Isn't the bail money in order?" Mom leaned forward, intent on the answer.

"Oh, yes. A runner from a messenger service brought it. It's just going to take time to track down who hired the messenger service, how many hands it went through, whose name is on the Seattle bank account; that kind of thing."

"Oh." Juli wrinkled her forehead. "If I remember right, Brett said he didn't have any family, at least around here."

"Brett Jones said a lot of things." Dad patted a yawn. He stood, stretched, and gave Mom a hand up. "What say we have a

51

prayer and hit the sack?"

Mom nodded, but Juli wondered how she could ever sleep. After the prayer, she snuggled down in bed with Clue nearby, picked up her journal, and wrote:

Just when it looked like everything was going to settle down, along comes more trouble. First, another bank robbery, at Sean's own bank. It is so scary, Lord. Second, two people are involved instead of just one. Third, Brett Jones gets out on bail from some apparently mysterious source. That's even more frightening. What if he tries to contact some of us?

She stared at the words, stark and terrifying against the white page. A hundred thoughts played hide-and-seek in her brain. After a time, she went on writing.

God, we all laughed when Shannon said we might have to go through what the Bible calls 'trials and revelations' (meaning tribulations, of course). It's hard to keep laughing with Brett out of jail. I know people are presumed innocent until proven guilty, but he confessed! What if he really is part of a crime ring? Who is the mysterious someone or ones willing to hand out that kind of money for such a bad risk? Are they so wealthy they don't care if Brett jumps bail and the money is forfeited?

She stopped again and absentmindedly reached over to pat Clue's soft cinnamon-brown fur. Her hand stopped in midair. A rush of fear climbed to her throat and made it hard to breathe. Suppose bail hadn't been posted as a favor to Brett Jones at all. What if it had been posted to keep him from identifying others involved in the series of robberies that had occurred in the West?

Juli shuddered. Brett might be in far more trouble out of jail than in. The masterminds behind such a plan could never be sure he wouldn't squeal on them. Juli released the death grip on her pencil and wrote:

Lord, I know Brett has done awful things, but You still love him. He can't be all bad, or he would never have taken Ted to the hospital after he hit him and ran. Please, don't let Brett get hurt. He needs to know You so much.

Juli put down her journal and pencil. Peace gradually crept over her. God was able to take care of her, her friends, even people like Brett if they would let Him. The best thing she or anyone could do was simply trust Him.

To Juli's disappointment, no further information about Brett's bail was forthcoming. The Paynes didn't stop by. If Dad knew anything, he kept it in the deep well of secrets his work as a police officer demanded. He did pass on one bit of news — the police had picked up Brett as a person of interest in the latest bank robbery but released him after questioning.

"He has a solid alibi," Dad admitted. "Some guy named Tod Markham vouched for him. Markham swore he and Jones drove to Vancouver, B.C. for the afternoon and didn't get back until late. We're checking Markham's background, of course."

Juli and Dave, Shannon and Ted talked about it over takeout burgers and shakes they carried to a sparsely populated park after a rousing tennis match a few days later. Juli hadn't mentioned the curious matter of the bail, but Brett's questioning and alibi were common knowledge. She felt no qualms about discussing them. "There's no way to prove or disprove his alibi," she said dejectedly. "With all the hundreds of people going back and forth daily from Washington State to Canada, no way would the customs

54

agents remember whether two certain guys crossed. Even if they did, they could come back through a different checkpoint and not be recognized."

Dave sipped his milkshake and slowly said, "Not unless they did something to call attention to themselves, which they wouldn't, even if they went to Canada."

"How can you sound so positive?" Juli teased, eager to see his face light up beneath his sun-bleached light brown hair.

"Elementary, my dear Watson," Dave said in his most Sherlock Holmes-like manner. "If they went to Vancouver, they wouldn't know there was a bank robbery or the need for an alibi." He looked pleased with himself and grinned broadly. "How's that for the Gilmore part of Scott and Gilmore, P.I.s?"

"Not bad," Ted praised. "Shannon, what great contribution do you have to help solve the mystery?" He finished his burger, crumpled the foil wrapping, and fired off a perfect two-point basket into a garbage container.

Her Irish eyes looked more blue than gray above her blue-flowered blouse. "Mercy me, I'm not a super sleuth like Juli and the rest of you! I just want those responsible caught and put in jail." She sighed.

"Cheer up." Ted patted her arm. "They

say lightning never strikes twice in the same place. Your dad's bank has had its robbery. It shouldn't happen again."

"Shouldn't doesn't mean it won't," she reminded him in a worried voice. "And lightning does strike twice in the same place. There are accounts on TV all the time telling about it. Is it okay if we talk about something else?"

"Sure." "Yeah." "All right."

"Good." She grinned at them. Excitement chased away her troubled expression. "Guess what? Molly Bowen called me just before you guys came. John Foster has the neatest idea! He didn't say anything before because he had to see if it would really work out. I mean, even though the older couple are Fosters, they are only distant relatives. Molly said John had to make sure it would be okay." The stone-cold dead silence following her jumbled announcement brought a peal of laughter.

"You all look like I came from Mars or something! Sorry. I'm blathering."

"Translate, will you please?" Ted pleaded.

"For certain." Shannon counted off items on her fingers. "One, John Foster's relatives live on an old farm near Birdsview. You know, the wide spot in the road between Sedro Woolley and Rockport. We pass it

56

when we go to the Skagit House." She giggled. "Birdsview is so small it isn't even on a map. Anyway, the only ones who live on the farm are Mr. and Mrs. Foster. They get lonesome and are totally thrilled at the idea of having people come for an all-day picnic."

"What people? What picnic?" Juli demanded.

Shannon tried to look innocent and failed miserably. The dancing light in her eyes showed how much fun it was to mystify her friends. "Seems like Sheerluck Holmes and Dr. What's-his-face should be smart enough to figure it out."

The others moaned. "Please! That's Sherlock and Dr. Watson."

Shannon relented. "All right." She put her hands around her mouth as if using a megaphone. Her voice turned tinny. "Hear ye, hear ye. Mr. and Mrs. Foster cordially invite our church youth group and all our Adopt-a-Grandparent senior adults who can make it, to spend Thursday next week at their farm. They are ecstatic about our coming." She clasped her hands. "It's going to be so loverly!"

"We can't give you a bad time about 'loverly.' It's from *My Fair Lady*," Juli put in. "The Birdsview trip sounds great. Did

57

Molly say whether John asked our youth leader about it?"

"Of course. Who do you think is working out the details? Kareem and Jasmine Thompson are as excited as the Fosters. So am I. Molly says it's wonderful out there, almost as peaceful as the Skagit House." A shadow flitted across her face and blotted out the happy anticipation. "We could use some peace, right?"

"Uh-huh." Juli's mind raced ahead. "Are we taking the church bus?"

"Plans aren't that settled yet. They will be at our meeting tonight. First, we have to see if the kids want to go. They'd better! It's a perfect way to get better acquainted with our Adopted Grandparents. They'll love it."

Chapter 5

Shannon nicknamed the Adopt-a-Grand-parent excursion Destination Birdsview. When Ted told her she meant *Operation* Birdsview, the Irish girl stubbornly shook her head. "We're for going to Birdsview, aren't we? That makes it our destination. Right?" Her friends reluctantly agreed.

The name stuck. John Foster presented Destination Birdsview to the church youth group at their Wednesday night meeting with such enthusiasm, the group unanimously voted to accept the Fosters' invitation. "You're going to love the farm," John explained, "It's a great place to hike. Not that we'll be running off and leaving our guests all day. But the folks plan to shoo us off for a time so they can get acquainted, too."

Brown-eyed Molly Bowen bounced on her chair and held up her hand to be recognized. "The nicest part is that we get to do something for others. Since we started the Adopt-a-Grandparent program I've wished we could share an intergenerational activity. Seniors have so much to offer! I could sit all day and listen to stories of when they were growing up."

A soft glow came to her freckled face. "It's so neat hearing what God has done in their lives. If it hadn't been for Him, some of them wouldn't have made it through the Great Depression. Or all the wars." Her eyes grew solemn. "It made me think how fortunate we are."

"I agree," Amy Hilton surprised everyone by saying. The petite, bottle-blond cheerleader wasn't known for thinking much about anyone except herself, or occasionally, her twin brother, Ted. Now she turned an unbecoming red. "Juli took me with her on one of her visits. I was shocked." She swallowed hard. "My own grandmother signed up! Ted goes to see her a lot, but I was so busy I hardly ever visited. Big mistake. We have a lot in common. I know Grandma will want to go. She's totally cool."

A giggle spilled out. "Someone asked her the other day how old she was. Know what Grandma said?" Amy giggled again. Not the everyone-look-at-me, high-pitched sound she used to attract attention, but a fun-filled laugh of pure enjoyment. "In Grandma's own words, and I quote, 'I'm sixty-one on the outside, and whatever age I choose to be at the moment on the inside!' Isn't that wild?"

Dave Gilmore grinned at Amy, then squeezed Juli's hand. "Sounds good to me," he said. "So does Destination Birdsview. This trip is going to be a riot." He turned to their youth leader, Kareem Thompson, who had been the only member of his family to survive a massacre in his native Africa. A missionary couple named Thompson rescued the boy, adopted him, and brought him to the United States. Now in his twenties, Kareem and his attractive wife Jasmine loved and served the Lord through working with youth and sharing their testimonies of what God had done in their lives. The youth group loved them.

"Are we taking the church bus?" Dave asked the handsome leader.

Kareem's teeth shone white against his dark skin. "Not this time," he replied. "We're asking parents who can get time off work to go as chaperones. It's roughly an hour's drive each way, and our adopted grandparents will be more comfortable in cars, vans, and station wagons. We want them as rested as possible so they can enjoy the farm and the Fosters."

His eyes twinkled with anticipation. "Ask your folks if they can go and let me know right away. Okay, who wants to head up the committees? We need callers to contact our group members who aren't here tonight, as well as our adopted grandparents. We'll need a food committee." His deep bass laugh broke out. "The Fosters wanted to provide everything. John and I said a flat and mighty *NO*. We finally convinced them they were to be our guests, even though we'll be at their farm. What about an entertainment committee?"

Juli raised her hand. "How long will we stay?"

Kareem looked surprised. "Until late afternoon. Why?"

"I was thinking of what Molly said. We usually have some kind of worship to close our outings. We could sing songs we all know, then just talk. A lot of our guests live alone. They don't always get a chance to share their experiences."

Shannon jumped up. "I don't know about the rest of you, but when Ted and I went visiting, our couple admitted they wondered whether young people cared anything about older people's lives." Several heads nodded in agreement and she went on. "When we invite our guests, why don't we ask them to come prepared to share a life experience they feel is significant and special, if they feel comfortable doing it. Maybe it will help us learn to stop, listen, and look a little more deeply inside other people."

Kareem joined in the laugh that swept through the room. "We usually say 'stop, look, and listen,' " he told Shannon. "This time, however, I feel you've said it a whole lot better than the person who first gave the advice."

Shannon pasted a silly smile on her face and shot Juli a triumphant look.

"Agreed?" Kareem asked. Hands unanimously shot into the air. "Good. That takes care of entertainment."

"I can hardly wait," Jasmine said in her soft voice. "The importance of storytelling is again being recognized throughout the world. I know we'll have great food and a beautiful setting for our Destination Birdsview, but we need to be aware there's something far more important here. The best gift we can give our adopted grandparents on our outing is the gift of *listening*." She smiled.

It didn't take long to form committees and finish the meeting. A short worship followed, then fresh peach cobbler topped with whipped cream appeared and won hearty approval and loud cheers. The meeting closed on a high note of excitement that carried Ted and Shannon, Dave and Juli, back to the Scotts.

The boys didn't come in, and Shannon bounced up the flower-edged walk to the porch with Juli close behind. The girls ran to the living room, piled onto the sofa, and eagerly told Mom and Dad about Destination Birdsview. Juli ended with, "You'll drive, won't you, Mom? Can you get the day off, Dad?"

Anne Scott nodded, but her husband ruefully shook his dark head. "Sorry. It sounds terrific, but I took so much leave to recuperate, this isn't a good time."

"My dad probably won't be able to go, either," Shannon put in. "He doesn't say much, but I guess things at the bank are really tense." Some of the evening's happiness left her animated face.

Juli saw the measured look Dad gave Mom. "What?" she blurted out.

"Another reason I can't make the trip is that I've arranged to take tomorrow off." He turned to Shannon. "I promised to take you to a trial. We haven't made it to an empty courtroom yet, but it's possible the Brett Jones trial may come sooner than we expect. I know you want to see what it's like, just in case."

64

"Wh-what kind of trial is it?" Shannon asked. Her hands clenched and she looked small and vulnerable sitting next to Juli.

"Nonpayment of child support. It shouldn't last long." Compassion showed in Gary Scott's gray eyes before he casually added, "How would you like to make it an assignment?" When they straightened and looked puzzled, he told them, "I just happened to mention our visit to an editor of the local paper. He promptly asked if you'd be willing to write up your impressions of what you see. No promises about it being published, but a good chance."

"You just happened to mention it?" Juli asked suspiciously.

He grinned. "You know how those things are."

Shannon's quickly raised eyebrows showed she saw straight through Dad's little scheme, but she said nothing. Juli suspected her father had deliberately made arrangements so her friend could focus on something other than the courtroom itself. "I think it's neat," she approved. "Can't you see it now, Shannon? Four-inch front page headlines screaming 'THURSDAY TRIAL,' followed by 'Observations of the American Justice System by Local Young Adult Authors Shannon Riley and Juli Scott.'"

She broke off and made a face. "Should I use my whole name? Julianne Scott. Sounds like a romance novelist, doesn't it?"

"You could save Julianne in case you someday decide to write Christian romance novels," Mom teased.

"At the risk of being mobbed, may I humbly suggest it is possible your article — if published — may not have four-inch headlines or make the front page?" Dad put in.

Juli waved aside his suggestion. "We will make it so good no editor can resist featuring it," she dreamed aloud. "Hey, do you think they'll include some author background information, telling about Shannon's winning contest entry?"

Her far-fetched ideas effectively relieved her friend's gloom, as Juli had known it would. Shannon began laughing and it carried over until bedtime. She also slept better than Juli. Concerned over her friend's reaction on the next day, Juli slept restlessly and awakened twice. Both times Shannon's even breathing showed she slept untroubled by bad dreams. Juli thankfully snuggled back in her bed and whispered a prayer all would go well at the trial.

Other than an initial anxious look around

66

the courtroom Thursday afternoon when the girls, Gary Scott, and Anne Scott arrived for the trial, Shannon did just fine. She found herself as caught up in the proceedings as Juli was. The plaintiff's sad story caught at her heart. The husband was obviously what society called a deadbeat dad, unwilling to support the two children he had fathered before divorce shattered still another family.

Shannon changed her mind when she heard the other side of the story. *I wouldn't pay child support, either, if I never got to see my children,* she indignantly thought. According to the defendant, every time he was supposed to have them, his ex-wife made other plans, or she and the children weren't home when he went to pick them up. No wonder he didn't want to give her money.

When the keen-eyed judge gave her ruling, Shannon sagged with relief. The father was to make payments but the mother must honor all visitation rights.

"Will she obey?" Shannon wanted to know when they left the courtroom.

"She'll be in big trouble if she doesn't." Dad's lips were set in a grim line. "I have no sympathy for real deadbeat dads, those who whine and skip out on their responsibilities. This man doesn't appear to be one of them.

I can't fault him for feeling if he's father enough to support his kids, he has the right to have them with him according to what was agreed on in the custody trial." His mouth relaxed. "Remember, you two. When you coauthor your masterpiece, don't get into the actual case or take sides. Just show how the American justice system offers each person involved the opportunity to be heard."

Several exciting and unexpected events followed the girls' interesting trial observation in rapid succession, all before Destination Birdsview.

Juli and Shannon wrote and polished their article, and Dad took it to his editor friend.

"Don't get your hopes up," Dad warned them. "This is what's called an evergreen article, one that isn't tied to a current event but can be used anytime. It may be held for weeks, possibly not printed at all."

"We know," they said, but privately agreed they didn't believe it!

Their faith paid off far sooner than they dreamed. A reporter missed a last-minute deadline and the article appeared on the Op-Ed page (opposite the Editorial page) of the Monday newspaper!

"It's wonderful!" Juli cried when her blondish-brown head and Shannon's dark one bent over the article. "Look at our names. Right there for the whole world to see and admire!"

"Well, Bellingham and Whatcom County, anyway," Shannon admitted. Her happy smile broadened. "Wonder if we will get any reactions?"

Seven congratulatory calls later, including one from the girls' ecstatic creative writing teacher, the phone rang again. Shannon answered. Her eyes widened. "What? Why . . ." She gulped. "I think you'd better speak with Juli." She held out the phone, looking as if she'd gone into shock.

Juli's stomach did a flip. She grabbed the phone. "This is Juli Scott." Her mouth dropped open. "You what? You do? *Tomorrow?* Of course. What time?" She frantically motioned for Shannon to hand her a pencil and scratch paper. "All right. No, it doesn't matter that you can only use one of us." She slowly hung up, blue eyes accusing. "Why didn't you warn me?"

"I was too surprised." Shannon shook her head, as if to clear away confusion.

"I still can't believe it," Juli breathed. "Talk about coincidences! A reporter misses a deadline. Our article gets published. A local TV host sees it. One of the kids scheduled to be on a peer discussion show cancels. The host needs a replacement. *Voilà!* One of us goes on live TV. *Tomorrow.*" Her heart pounded.

"What do you mean one of us?" Shannon jerked back and held out both hands as if holding off an attack. "It is absotively, posilutely not going to be me!"

"Why not? You wrote the article just as much as I did." Juli felt forced to say it, even though her traitorous, thumping heart screamed how much she wanted to be the coauthor who appeared on the show.

"Forget it. I'd be so scared I'd fall heels over head and make a total fool of myself before I ever got on stage," Shannon said. "You'll do a great job, Juli." Complete faith in her friend's ability underlined each word.

Juli didn't have the heart to correct the Rileyism to head over heels. Thrilled at the idea, she laughed and deliberately made one of her own. "Flattery will get you everywhere," she said. "Oh, Shannon, this is so exciting! It's live, too."

"I know. I'll be right there in the studio audience." Now that she was off the hook, her eyes shone with pleasure. So did Mom and Dad's when they heard the news. Juli and Shannon spent the rest of the day choosing outfits. They decided on simple summer skirts and tops. "My favorite author advises never wearing anything brand-new to an interview or speaking engagement," Shannon said. "That way you won't be thinking about your clothes."

All Juli thought about was how scared she was! Yet once seated in a semicircle around the host, she concentrated on giving the best answers she could. The show went well and Juli enjoyed herself immensely. "I didn't even think about the thousands of people who might be watching," she said afterward.

One of those thousands followed up in a terrifying manner. Thursday morning when Gary Scott started for work, he found an envelope with the typed words JULIE SCOTT on it taped to the front door of the house. He brought it to Juli and teased, "Which of your friends can't spell your name right?"

"I don't know." Juli slit the envelope, read the message, and silently held out the single page so her parents could see it. Boldface words warned: DON'T TESTIFY AGAINST BRETT JONES. A crude skull and crossbones followed.

Chapter 6

Anne Scott stared at the horrid words on the paper her daughter still held: DON'T TESTIFY AGAINST BRETT JONES. The skull and crossbones just underneath the message made it even uglier. "Oh," Anne burst out. "It's a death threat!" She put one hand to her throat as if she found it hard to breathe. "The skull and crossbones are just like those used on the bank robbery notes."

Dad took the page and examined it. "Not really. Those were hand drawn. This is a computer graphic. The message is also computer generated. No typewriter ever came up with this particular style."

Juli fought the fear springing up within her and managed to say, "May I see it again, please?" Dad handed her the threatening note, and she concentrated on the broad, dark letters. "The style of the letters looks familiar. I think we may have it on our computer." Excitement stirred. "If we can identify the font, we'll have a clue."

"Great minds do run together," Dad

praised. "I was thinking the same thing. Come on, Detective Scott. We have work to do. I'll call the Paynes and ask them to meet me. Not here. Shannon will be coming soon. I do want them to see this before I turn it over to the prosecuting attorney." He smiled at Juli. "Now let's see what the computer will tell us."

For one of the few times in Juli's life, she saw her mother lose control. Anne Scott's eyes darkened to midnight-blue. "This is a death threat, not some magazine mystery to be solved!" she said in a high-pitched voice. "Juli's in danger and you two sit there talking about computer graphics and fonts and clues. I just can't take it!" She dropped her head into her hands. Tearing sobs shattered the deathly quiet room.

Juli couldn't move. She felt she had fallen into a trance. This couldn't be happening. Mom didn't act like this. Ever. She never had. Not when Dad was missing and presumed dead. Not when Shannon disappeared. Not even when Dad ended up in the hospital and they didn't know what the future held for him.

The next instant Gary Scott had Mom in his arms. "I'm sorry," he told her. "It's just that anything we discover to help us find out who sent this note means this will be over that much sooner."

"I know." Mom clung to him. Her voice sounded muffled against his shirt. "I'm sorry, too, for getting so upset." She stopped crying and looked into Dad's eyes. Her smile reminded Juli of a glorious rainbow after a drenching storm.

"You're a real trouper, Anne," Dad said huskily. He dropped a quick kiss on her upturned face. "No man could ask for a braver or better wife."

She sniffled and slid from his encircling arms. "Thanks. I'll go wash my face." Her lips trembled, but the peace Juli counted on seeing in her mother's face had already begun to return. "Get on with your sleuthing." She walked toward the bathroom, head high and shoulders squared.

"That is one courageous woman," Dad said. "It's a lot harder to be the one on the sidelines when there's danger than to be involved."

Shannon's special *rat-a-tat-tat* sounded at the front door. As usual, she opened it without waiting for an invitation and called, "I'm here." The sound of her steps coming toward the dining room broke the fragile moment of understanding and appreciation between father and daughter.

Between the knock and the time Shannon

reached the kitchen, Juli hastily slid the note and envelope into the pocket of her jeans. She pulled the tail of her white tee shirt out of the waistband of her jeans and let it hang over her leather belt. It hid the bulge the paper made and Juli prayed it wouldn't crackle. The last thing Shannon needed right now was to learn about the death threat.

"Aren't you ready yet?" the Irish girl demanded when she reached the dining room. Like Juli, she wore comfortable sneakers and jeans, but a green tee shirt. Her eyes sparkled and a big smile made Juli more determined than ever not to destroy her friend's happiness until absolutely necessary.

"Well?" Shannon demanded impatiently. "Are you going to stand there until you're gray and old? There's a picnic waiting, remember?"

"It's old and gray, not gray and old," Juli mumbled. She cast a despairing glance at Dad. He could call the Paynes from the car phone, but how was she to check the message against their computer, with Shannon impatiently tapping her fingers on the back of a chair and urging her to hurry?

Gary Scott rose to his daughter's wordless appeal. He turned to Shannon and smiled. "I'd have thought by now you would have another car. What's wrong? Can't you talk Sean into a brand-new convertible?"

Under cover of Shannon's explanation that they hadn't seen a car which suited both of them, Juli hurried to the den. She turned on the computer, resenting every second it took until she could call up the word processing program. A hasty scan of the font styles confirmed the note had been done using Impact. Was it to carry the added message that the sender meant exactly what the skull and crossbones implied? She shuddered, started to close, then paused and listened.

The rumble of Dad's voice and Shannon's merry laugh would buy Juli some time. She clicked on Insert, called up Pictures, and scanned the list. No skull and crossbones. Conscious of her dwindling time, she switched to Symbol. The Milestones category offered no help, so she went to Wingdings.

A tiny skull and crossbones identical to the one on the threatening note leered at her from between a bomb and a pennant. "Bingo!" No time remained to print out a copy, so Juli rapidly went through the steps to end her Windows session.

Few things on earth had ever looked more beautiful to her than the printed message:

"You can now safely turn off your computer." Relief flooded her and she pushed buttons. Before the screen went blank, she had already grabbed a small self-adhesive sheet. She scribbled "Word for Windows Impact Wingdings." Sticking it on the envelope with her name misspelled, Juli shoved the whole thing into a nine by twelve manila envelope and carried it to the kitchen.

"Dad hasn't gone, has he?" she breathlessly asked Mom, who was helping Shannon pack potato salad and fresh fruit in an ice chest.

Anne Scott's gaze fastened on the envelope. "He's just now backing out."

Juli raced through the kitchen door into the garage and on into the driveway. Mom's voice floated after her. "Isn't it funny how even the most organized men sometimes forget things?"

Juli grinned. Mom hadn't actually said Dad forgot anything. She was getting as adept at telling nothing as her husband and daughter. "Hey, Dad. Wait up!" Juli waved the envelope and galloped toward the street.

He braked, reached through the window, open to the early morning air, and glanced at the envelope. Juli nodded to show him she'd found their first clue. "Good girl," he whispered, before raising his voice so it could be clearly heard if Shannon or Mom came outside. "Thanks, pal. What would I do without you?"

Juli lingered long enough to watch him round the corner a few blocks away. Her body turned and walked back to the house, but she mentally went with him. Dad would meet Andrew and Mary safely away from curious eyes. They'd examine the death threat, double-check Juli's computer information, and turn the note and envelope over to the district attorney. If only she could be there! *You can't,* she told herself sternly. *You also can't let on anything's wrong. This day is too important to a lot of people for you to spoil it.*

The feeling she wasn't a good enough actress to carry it off gnawed at her. A quick prayer for help before going back inside helped some, but a cold hard knot of fear remained, and her hands felt clammy. Could she do it?

She stepped into the kitchen and found her answer in her mother's untroubled eyes. Their understanding flash told Juli that Anne Scott had gone straight to her heavenly Father in prayer. A rush of love and admiration filled Juli. She hugged Mom and felt some of the pressing weight slide onto the strong shoulders beneath her arms. How true it was that sharing a burden cut it in half.

Obviously unaware of the undercurrent beneath the Scotts' calm, Shannon happily said, "We couldn't have asked for a more perfect day. All green and gold and blue." She wrinkled her nose. "I hope our adopted grandparents slept better than I did last night." Without waiting for a response she admitted, "I'm always like that when the next day is going to be unusual."

"Me, too," Juli said. "I —" A ring of the telephone cut her off. She sprang to answer it. "Hello? You can't? Why?" A long silence followed, then her face brightened. "Don't be silly. Bring her. There won't be a problem. The kids won't care and our guests will be charmed. Okay. See you soon."

"Which means?" Mom prompted. In white jeans and her favorite red shirt, she looked more like Juli's older sister than her mother.

"The Gilmores have some kind of mix-up about Christy. Dave's dad and mom have an out-of-town business appointment today. They didn't realize Dave wouldn't be around to stay with Christy and it's too late to line up another sitter. He was going to cancel until I told him to bring her along. That's okay, isn't it?"

"Of course," Shannon agreed. "Christy is so well-behaved, everyone likes her. She also looks enough like Dave to be his twin, if she were sixteen instead of eight." She checked her watch. "We'd better hurry. Everyone's supposed to meet at the church so we can go caravan style."

A half hour later, Dave opened the door of the Riley van Sean had graciously lent for the occasion. Christy stood just behind her big brother, looking more like him than ever. Both wore jeans and high-top basketball shoes. Christy's spotless yellow tee shirt and blond ponytail shone in the sun. Dave's tanned face above his white tee shirt stretched in a broad grin.

"Hi, Dave. Hi, Christy. Glad you could come." Juli hugged the little girl and she blushed with pleasure. "We're counting on you to help our guests have a good time. Is that okay with you?"

Christy squared her shoulders importantly. Her ponytail switched up and down when she nodded. "Sure." She slid a well-scrubbed hand into Juli's and skipped beside her toward the gathering crowd of vehicles. "I like old people. I'm going to be one of them someday and tell stories of the olden days, like Dave says they're going to do today."

Juli didn't dare look at Shannon, who choked and hurried toward Ted. "Right. In the meantime, let's see what's happening." She looked up and caught a curious expression in Dave's blue eyes. It made her heartbeat quicken, especially when he glanced at his sister then back at Juli. "What are you thinking?" she asked after Christy deserted her and ran toward Kareem and Jasmine Thompson.

Dave grinned maddeningly. "Stick around a few years and I may tell you."

Had the thought crossed his mind that if he and Juli someday married they might have a little girl who looked a lot like Christy? Juli felt her cheeks warm at the idea and scrambled for safer ground. She was Dave's girl *pro tem* (for the time being). Only God knew the future, and He unrolled it one day at a time. Thank goodness. She wanted to enjoy every one of those days and not get hung up on tomorrow's maybes. "Right now we need to get going."

"Okay, fellow investigator. Anything new on our latest case?" Dave caught her hand and swung it, much as Christy had done.

Juli weighed the value of keeping quiet against the overwhelming need for more support than Mom could give, because she was more closely involved. Dad wouldn't mind if she swore Dave to secrecy and told him. "Bend your head down so no one else can hear," she whispered. He obeyed without question. It was one of his traits she liked most. No questions. No arguments. Just instant recognition she wouldn't ask him to do something unless it were important.

In the fewest words possible, she told him about the note marked JULIE. He grunted but said nothing. Juli filled him in on the menacing message inside and how she traced it to Impact and Wingdings on the computer. "Don't mention it to anyone else," she finished. "Especially Shannon." She bit her lip. "I hate keeping things from her, but there's no sense giving her anything new to worry about. Our courtroom visit last Thursday helped her feel better about the trial."

Dave stepped back and stared at her. "Maybe you need to make that plural."

"What do you mean?"

"You've had more than one trial on Thursday. Last week, the real thing. Today, another kind of trial." He took a deep breath and his eyes darkened. "I don't want to frighten you, but did you ever think attending the trial may have started a whole chain of trouble?"

"I follow. If we hadn't gone, we wouldn't have written it up. The newspaper wouldn't have printed the article. I wouldn't have been on TV." She grabbed his arm. "Do you think whoever left the note saw me on that program?"

Christy raced toward them and Dave only had time to say, "I don't know. It may not even be related, but there are a lot of crazies out there. Be careful, Juli, and remember: I'm here for you anytime you need me." A quick squeeze of her hand emphasized the promise. It also made Juli feel a whole lot better.

In a short time, everyone found their assigned places. Kareem Thompson facetiously called, "Wagons, ho!" Destination Birdsview began. Each vehicle held laughing youth group members, parents, and adopted grandparents. Juli lay aside everything but the special day, singing and laughing with the rest.

When they reached the Fosters' farm, she stepped from the van and forgot troubles, grandparents, even Christy, who danced beside her. A spreading valley stretched before her. Mountains lined one side, etched against the sky. One ridge looked like a sleeping giant lying on his back. A white-painted, old but well-kept two-story farmhouse snuggled against a smaller, sloping green hillside on the opposite side of the valley. Its windows and porch offered a magnificent view. A picturesque, unpainted barn crouched on the ground to the right, with another barely visible farmhouse on the left.

Hayfields and pastureland with cows and horses lay between the house and the mountain ridge. A silvery stream lazily flowed through the valley. Heavy old growth timber began just back of the barn on the right side of the house and climbed steeply for what must be miles.

Juli found her troubles slinking into a dark corner of her brain, defeated by the tranquillity around her. If only all of life could be as beautiful as this part of God's creation! She whispered, "Lord, is even heaven more peaceful?"

Juli felt the mountains, stream, and valley held out welcoming arms to her. And that she had come home after a long and troublesome journey.

Chapter 7

"If I live to be older than old sleeping giant up there, I'll never forget today," Juli told Shannon an hour after the Destination Birdsview caravan arrived at the Foster farm. The girls stood on the porch, overlooking the front yard, mountains, and valley. "Just look." She waved at the lawn below. "They look like they have lived here forever."

"For certain." Shannon's gaze followed Juli's pointing finger. All ages mingled. Some strolled toward the pasture. Others wandered to the stream. A few braved black-berry thorns and filled their mouths with warm, juicy berries. Still others were content to sit in lawn chairs and simply talk.

Mr. and Mrs. Foster fit into the scene like apple slices between two layers of pie crust. Mr. Foster sought out and attended to anyone standing or sitting alone. His wife bustled after him like a happy caboose following an engine. Laughter and the clink of horseshoes floated up to the girls. Some of the guests had staged an impromptu tournament.

"It makes you wish you could stay here forever, doesn't it?" Shannon softly asked. She turned her shining gaze from the scene below to Juli. "It's also for remindin' me of Ireland." She looked across at the mountains that jutted up into the sky. Mrs. Foster had shown them where some ridges down below the sleeping giant looked like a lady's profile. "Especially the Killarney region in southwest Ireland. It's known for its mountains and lakes. We must be for goin' one day."

Touched by what Shannon said, Juli laid her hand on her friend's arm and nodded. She searched for the right words, but before she could find them, John Foster shouted from below, "Come on, lazybones. We have two hours before it's time to put on the feedbag. Who's going to tackle yon hill with me?" He pointed to the steeply sloping rise beyond the barn. "There's an old logging road and a bunch of trails." He grinned. "I'll play Daniel Boone and be your guide."

"Heaven help us," Dave Gilmore told him. His sister jumped up and down and was first to volunteer. "I'll go. I mean, if Dave says it's okay."

"Hear ye, hear ye, surely the rest of you won't be outdone by this courageous child?" John bellowed. "Gather 'round, folks. It's climb-the-mountain time."

"You sound more like Kermit the Frog than Daniel Boone," Ted Hilton said.

Encouraged by the laugh that followed, Dave jeered, "You think it will take us two hours to climb that hill?"

This time Mr. Foster chuckled. "It might and then again, it might not. Appearances can be deceiving." His eyes twinkled.

"Is he joking, Mrs. Foster?" Shannon called to their hostess.

"It's steeper than it looks," she admitted. "Besides, there are places you'll want to stop and look across to the mountains and down into the valley. There's also a river in a canyon. Take your time. The rest of us will visit and have some fresh lemonade while you're gone." The corners of her eyes crinkled in a way that showed she was no stranger to laughter. "I don't suppose you young folks care for any just now."

"Do we ever!" John grabbed his throat and pretended to stagger. "Drink up, everyone. That way, we'll be prepared in case we get lost."

Mr. Foster snorted. "Fine Daniel Boone you'll make! Don't pay any attention to him, folks. He's hiked that hill enough times to keep from leading you astray."

"Are there wild animals?" Amy asked

from her position on a blanket.

"The coyotes do a lot of barking at night, but chances are, you won't see one. As a rule, they're pretty wary," Mrs. Foster said. "There are birds and squirrels. You may see a deer, although they like to lie under the trees where it's cool during the warm part of the day. As for bears —"

"Bears!" Amy leaped to her feet.

Ted rolled his eyes at his sister and turned to Mrs. Foster. "You were saying before you were so rudely interrupted?"

"It isn't likely you'll see one," their hostess comforted.

Amy made a face and dropped back on her blanket. "It would be just our luck for a half-dozen bears to be around. I'll stay and spend time with Grandma."

"It will have to be while we're climbing, Goldilocks," her peppery grandmother told her. "I may not quite reach the top, but I intend to tackle that hill while I'm still young enough to have a fighting chance!"

Shouts of laughter greeted her announcement and a few other senior adults declared their intention of climbing with the younger people.

"Come on, Amy. I'll protect you." Carlos Ramirez, newest addition to the youth group, held out his hand. His teeth flashed white in his smooth, olive-skinned face. Short, curly black hair topped a strong, muscular body.

Shannon nudged Juli, who stiffened. Amy had been the first girl in her class to decide boys were interesting people, not just creatures who usually ran faster and climbed higher than girls. Ever since, the pretty blond had concentrated exclusively on those who could help boost her popularity. How would she respond to the son of migrant workers? Even a handsome young man whose laughing black eyes held a great deal of admiration when he looked at her?

Juli thought of Carlos's story. Kareem and Jasmine had discovered him when he dropped in at a youth rally in Mount Vernon. His keen intelligence and wistful longing for more learning than he could get while moving from place to place following the crop seasons touched the Thompsons' hearts. A great deal of serious discussion followed. So did intense prayer by Kareem, Jasmine, and the parents, who wanted a better life for their children than they could provide. At last the Ramirezes agreed to let Carlos stay with the Thompsons for the following school year. They also agreed their son should move to Bellingham immediately. Kareem and Jasmine would have

Carlos tested to see in what areas he needed special help. If it proved more than they could give, they would find a tutor.

Principal S. Miles — Mr. Smiles, as the students called him — was delighted by the opportunity for Hillcrest High to become more multicultural. He arranged for the tests and called Carlos and the Thompsons to his office the moment he received the results.

"Carlos, you are reading at a college freshman level," Mr. Smiles announced joyfully. "And you're at high school junior level in mathematics and social studies. Your only weakness is science. But don't worry. If you're willing to work hard for the rest of the summer, we'll enroll you as a probationary junior. You will have to take extra science courses on the side."

"*Si.* I mean, yes. I will work hard and make you all proud."

Carlos tackled science like a football team tackles a practice dummy. A well-pleased Mr. Smiles quoted the college student tutor a few days later as saying he had never seen anyone so willing and eager to learn. Carlos's excellent reading ability, gained by forcing sleepy eyes to remain open after long days of grueling work, served him well. Juli noticed that in the short time he'd been there, Carlos listened carefully to what Kareem taught the senior high students, and to Pastor Johnson's sermons. She believed Carlos would invite Christ into his heart soon.

Now she silently prayed, *Please, God, don't let Amy act snobbish. Carlos is too nice to be hurt.* She relaxed when the petite cheerleader blushed, took the helping hand, and sprang lightly to her feet.

"Mercy me," Shannon hissed. "She acts as if she likes him. Will I never cease to wonder?"

"You mean, 'Will wonders never cease,' but it's okay your way, too," Juli generously told her as they started toward the others.

"What a complete face about it would be if Amy started liking Carlos," Shannon said when Ted and Dave met them at the head of the path that wound to a fenced pasture. An old road on the opposite side led to an inviting shaded trail.

"It's 'about face' for *you*," Ted told her when he could stop laughing. "Put your Rileyisms into low gear. We have a hard climb ahead." He added, admiration in his voice, "Hey, look at Grandma go. She's more than keeping up with Carlos and Amy."

Juli didn't expect to have any trouble

climbing. She stayed in good physical condition by playing tennis, swimming, and skiing. Yet by the time they reached the top, she found herself panting. Mrs. Foster had been right about the trail being steep. Juli and the others, including Grandma Hilton, wisely kept what Shannon called a "steady but slow pace."

Frequent stops to rest also paid off. Although some straggled, all of the party eventually reached the top. It was worth it. The valley floor lay so far below, Juli had the sensation of viewing it from an airplane. By unspoken agreement, silence swept through the group. For a long time, the hikers simply sat and watched the shifting patterns made by clouds that appeared close enough to touch.

Christy Gilmore's smudged yellow tee shirt bore mute evidence of sweaty hands and lack of a tissue to wipe them dry. The end of a leafy crown she had fashioned from ivy and stuck on her head, trailed. She sat still as long as she could, then suggestively patted her stomach. "I wish I had a sandwich." She eyed Dave and hinted more strongly. "Or some of the Thompsons' fried chicken and Juli's potato salad." Her blue eyes gleamed. "Guess what Mrs. Foster has for dessert? Homemade strawberry shortcake! She said I could help her butter the shortcake biscuits when they come out of the oven, and help her whip the cream."

Dave groaned hungrily and Juli's stomach gave a sympathetic grumble. She hadn't realized how starved she felt until Christy started talking about food. The very thought of strawberry shortcake made her mouth water.

John looked at his watch. "You have the right idea, Your Hungriness. It's time for us to start back." He stood, grabbed Molly Bowen's hand, and raised her to her feet. "Are you okay?" he asked Grandma Hilton.

She smirked. "I made it up the mountain. I can make it back down." To prove it, she tossed her head, said "Come along, Amy," and started down the trail with the pack of hungry hikers close at her heels.

"I never saw so much food," Christy whooped when the disheveled group reached the farmhouse. Her wide-open eyes resembled blue dinner plates.

"It looks like a Walton family reunion," Dave told her. "Someone has been busy. Hey, Kareem. How come you didn't wait for us to set up?"

Their leader grinned. "I had plenty of

help." He waved toward tables made by placing sheets of plywood over old sawhorses, then spreading tablecloths on top. "Juli's mother, the Fosters, and several of our guests suggested we surprise you. I suggest you all get washed up."

Christy and Juli splashed together and shared the same towel. "Can I tell you something private?" the little girl asked.

Juli resisted the urge to tell her she should say "may," not "can." Correcting Shannon was one thing. Telling this earnest-faced child she didn't say something right was a different story. "Anytime."

Christy planted slightly grubby hands on her hips. "I'm sure with all the grown-ups here they won't ask me to say the blessing. If they did, I wouldn't just thank God for the day and the food. I'd thank Him that a bear didn't get us up on the mountain. Then I'd thank Him for the chicken and potato salad and pickles and corn on the cob."

She looked like a small blond angel when she said, "Most of all, I'd thank Him for the strawberry shortcake I get to help make. Oh, I'd thank Him for you, too, Juli. I'm glad you're Dave's protein girl." She importantly added, "That means 'for a time.'"

"You sound like Shannon," Juli accused between giggles. "It's *pro tem,* and it does

94

mean 'for a time.' " She smoothed Christy's tangled ponytail. "I'm glad, too."

"So am I." A deep voice made both girls jump.

Juli felt herself blush, but Christy said sternly, "It's not p'lite to sneak up on ladies when they're talking. Mom says so and she knows everything." She stuck out her lower lip, daring either of them to disagree.

Dave promptly grabbed her and swung her to his shoulder. "Sorry. Just for that I'll find you the biggest drumstick on the platter."

Christy squealed. "David Allen Gilmore, put me down!" She sounded so like a scolding mother Juli had to turn away to hide a laugh. Christy also puffed up like a yellow balloon after midday dinner, when everyone present solemnly agreed they'd never eaten better strawberry shortcake. "I s'pect someday I'll make some man a good wife," she told them, so serious no one dared laugh until her brother quickly added, "I s'pect you will," and offered her the last delicious bite of his treasured dessert.

The merry group took a break while the youth group cleaned up the dishes and stored leftovers in the refrigerator. "Be thinking of your stories," Kareem told the adopted grandparents after everyone regrouped. Several smiled; all looked eager.

"I'll bet they stayed awake last night planning what to share," Amy whispered to Juli when they found themselves next to each other with the Fosters and Amy's grandmother on either side of them. "This is the best activity we've ever had." She raised her voice so everyone could hear. "Hey, what do you say we make this an annual event? I mean, if it's all right with the Fosters."

"Great idea," Carlos heartily approved. "My year will be up, but may I come back for our reunion, please?" His black eyes sparkled at Amy.

Again soft color stole to Amy's face. And again Juli wondered if Amy really did like the new boy. How would it affect her popularity with the kids at school who stuck together and thought they were so cool? Could someone who cared so much about being liked give up her position? Mr. Smiles made a big thing about Hillcrest being one big happy family. Yet cliques continued, and Carlos wouldn't be welcomed by some of Amy's friends.

Molly Bowen led the group in some rousing songs that required Juli's attention. Molly's freckles shone like newly minted pennies. Juli hadn't realized how much bounce the redheaded girl possessed.

"She'd make a good cheerleader," Amy whispered. The honest admiration for the girl who had stolen John Foster's attention away from Amy surprised Juli. She couldn't wait to tell Shannon there must be more to Amy than bleached blond hair.

The other girl's obvious interest in the older people's experiences confirmed it. So did the sparkling drops on Amy's eyelashes when the group sang "God Be with You" in closing. She whispered through trembling lips, "It's hard to sing about meeting in heaven. Some of our adopted grandparents are really old. We may not meet them again until we get there."

Juli gave Amy the first sincere hug ever. "I know. I —"

A loud cry from the edge of the woods cut off the rest of her sentence.

Chapter 8

Before the echoes of the cry died, another came, louder and more frightened. Dave leaped from his place, his face now pale despite its tan. "Christy?"

"Dave, where are you?" The child's wail tore at Juli's heart. Dave's long legs were already carrying him to the dense stand of trees at the edge of the Fosters' property. A dozen other youth group members thundered close behind, with Kareem and Carlos in the lead.

Juli fought the paralyzing fear that threatened to freeze her to the spot, and ran over the uneven ground. God wouldn't allow anything to happen to a trusting child like Christy! He couldn't. She heard Shannon panting beside her. Amy stumbled just behind, sobbing with every step.

A white-faced little girl burst from behind a clump of bushes and raced toward the rescuers. Dave dropped to a kneeling position, held out his arms, and braced himself for her weight. Seconds later, Christy flung herself against her brother and burst into noisy tears.

"Are you hurt?" Dave hoarsely demanded. He quickly checked arms and legs.

Christy shook her head violently. "No," she said, burrowing her face into his chest. "The man. That awful man," she wailed.

Juli turned to stone. Surely Christy hadn't been gone long enough for someone to hurt her! It seemed only a minute ago that she was standing by Grandma Hilton's chair talking with her.

Dave gripped his little sister's arms. "What man, Christy? *What did he do?*"

"H-he spied on me." Terror shone in the clear blue eyes. She pointed toward the woods. "Mrs. Thompson said we'd be leaving soon. I wanted to explore a little bit more before we left . . ." She swiped at her tearstained face and left a long dirty streak across one cheek. Her whole body shook.

"Don't be scared. I won't let anyone get you." Dave's ragged voice turned deadly and his mouth set in a grim line.

Mrs. Foster pushed her way through the crowd; she was breathing hard and looked worried. "Where's my favorite kitchen helper? My goodness, child. We thought you were badly hurt. What happened?"

Christy huddled closer to Dave and

looked up with drenched blue eyes. "A man looked at me. He hid behind a big bunch of trees and looked at me."

"A man! In our woods? Are you sure?"

The tousled head bobbed violently. "Right over there." She pointed toward the huge stand of trees from which she had run.

"Did he say anything, or touch you?" A white line formed around Dave's lips.

"No. He just stood and stared like he hated me. Dave, why did he do that? I never saw him before. Never ever." She began to cry again.

Dave signaled to the others with lifted eyebrows. "Check it out, okay?"

"Sure. You girls and women wait here," Kareem ordered. Half the group headed for the spot Christy had pointed out.

Dave stood with his sister in his arms. "How about getting you back to the house and cleaned up?" he said. "All those tears are going to drown you." A faint giggle rewarded his efforts at cheering her up.

"I wouldn't be a bit surprised to find an extra piece of shortcake," Mrs. Foster volunteered. "Anyone want it?"

Being frightened by a stranger couldn't compete with shortcake Christy had helped make. "Me," a small voice said.

"Well, good. I do hate to see it go to waste.

Besides, any girl who helped make it with her very own hands deserves another piece." Mrs. Foster smiled at Christy. "If you come with me, Dave can help the others search for the man you saw. The idea! Coming on private property and scaring guests. I can tell you this, Miss Christy Gilmore, he'd better watch his step or we'll fix him."

Christy slid from Dave's arms and trustingly took Mrs. Foster's kindly hand. "What will we do to him?"

"Hmm. What do you think we should do?"

"We should say, 'Go away and stop scaring little girls. No shortcake for *you*,'" Christy solemnly announced. She skipped along beside her new friend, ponytail bouncing with every step.

Dave ran toward the woods and Juli swallowed a half-laugh, half-sob. "How quickly the promise of a treat took the horror from Christy's day! Now when she remembers the man, the edge of fear will be dulled by a wise woman's quick actions," she said to Shannon in a low voice. "I'm not sure I can say the same."

"What do you mean?" Her friend tore her gaze from the direction in which the men and boys had gone and looked puzzled.

Way to go, Juli silently scolded herself.

Used to sharing everything with Shannon, she'd forgotten the decision not to mention that morning's threatening note. Besides, a child seeing someone in the woods miles from Bellingham couldn't be related to a sicko who sent death threats, could it?

She licked her lips at the awful thought and scrambled for an explanation. "When Christy screamed, my knees turned to jelly. It amazes me I could even move. Thank God she's all right."

"What I can't understand is why or how anyone knew she'd be there," Shannon slowly replied. She clutched Juli's arm. "It's almost as though the man lay in wait hoping to catch her alone. Why would he do that? How could he even know she would be here?"

Not her. Me, thought Juli. For a moment, Juli was afraid she had spoken the words aloud. She hadn't, for Shannon didn't answer. Her imagination went wild. What if the creep who left the note had followed the van to the church, then trailed the caravan from Bellingham? *Ridiculous,* Juli told herself.

Reason hammered against the wish to write the idea off. It would be easy enough for someone to do. She and her friends had no reason to be suspicious. They wouldn't have noticed any particular car behind them. When the caravan came to the lane leading into the Fosters' place, a follower could simply drive on by, park the car, and come back.

No way. There isn't that much tree cover between here and the main road, part of Juli's mind protested. She had to admit, however, that with everyone busy and having a good time, a person might have slipped in unobserved. Even if those in the barely visible farmhouse to the left of the Fosters' saw the stranger, they would think he was one of the guests.

"I wish the boys and men would come," Shannon remarked.

"So do I." Juli stared at the thicket where they had disappeared. No leaves rustled. No movement hinted anyone or anything had recently disturbed them. Five minutes struggled by . . . ten . . . fifteen. Voices reached the waiting group. The search party came into sight and toward the girls and Grandma Hilton.

"Well?" she demanded.

Kareem Thompson shook his head. His dark eyes looked serious. "A few footprints but they could have been made by anyone or anything. The same for broken branches." He turned to Dave. "I don't doubt Christy's word. She either saw a man or thought she did. Is she overly imaginative?"

Dave shook his head. "No more than most kids."

"I don't think she imagined it," Juli burst out. "Christy just wanted to explore. She had no reason to believe she'd meet anyone."

"I agree," Amy said unexpectedly. "She was too terrified for it to have been her imagination. She also said the man spied on her. He stood behind the trees and looked at her as if he hated her. Why would a happy child like Christy even think such a thing if it weren't true?"

Carlos sent her a look of admiration. "Good question." He sighed. "I just wish we could have found more to go on."

Juli searched her mind, trying to remember clearly. Had she subconsciously heard the sound of a motor on the highway, a car starting, anything out of the ordinary? No. The distance in from the main road dimmed sounds. If her earlier theory was correct and someone had trailed her to the farm, he had left no clues.

"We need to start back to Bellingham," Kareem told the subdued group.

"We also don't want to spoil the day for our guests," Dave warned.

Rebellion filled Juli. She stayed behind when her friends started to the house.

"All right, what is it?" Dave asked.

Juli glanced from his concerned blue eyes to the soft ground beneath her feet. She viciously dug the toe of one sneaker into the earth, not caring how grimy it became. "What right do creeps have to ruin everything that's beautiful?" she choked out. "The farm seemed so peaceful, so far away from crime and sin and ugliness. Yet a little girl can't even walk in the woods a couple of hundred yards from the house without being frightened!"

Dave dropped one arm across her shoulders and gave her a little hug. "I know what you mean. It seems impossible bad things can happen here. Or at the Skagit House. Yet people choose to do wrong. Those choices affect all of us."

"It isn't fair." Her anger spilled into the quiet air.

"I know," Dave said again. He sounded tired and a whole lot older than sixteen. "We can't change the world, Juli. We *can* change *our* world, by standing for what's right and not being afraid to speak out. Every time anyone says no to drugs, booze, and all the other garbage out there, it makes the world a little better place. God's still in control of the world, but He expects us to help, right?" Dave gave an embarrassed laugh. "Sorry. I didn't mean to preach."

Most of Juli's anger drained away at his serious words. "You aren't. Thanks. Sometimes I need to be reminded."

Dave squeezed her shoulders again, then dropped his arm and took her hand. "Come on, better half of Scott and Gilmore, P.I.s. Let's go see what other 'trials and revelations' this Thursday has in store for us — quoting Shannon, of course."

She groaned. "Don't even mention the possibility. I don't see how much more can go wrong today."

"Is that one of your hunch-type premonitions?" Dave teased. "Or a prayer?"

"Whatever." She motioned with her free hand.

When they reached the edge of the lawn, Dave stopped her. "Look back," he whispered. "The peace is still here. Remember it this way, okay?"

Hand in hand they gazed from woods to valley, from shining stream to mountain peaks etched against the sky. Juli gradually recaptured the peace she had rebelled against losing. It grew during the farewell prayer Mr. Foster pronounced on the group. She clung to it with both hands on the drive to Bellingham. At the church parking lot, the groups came together again so everyone had a ride home. A chorus of "thank you's" and "what a wonderful day" rang in her ears when Mom turned the Riley van with Juli and Shannon toward home.

"The day was practically perfect," Shannon happily announced. "Except for Christy's spy."

Juli's good mood vanished like Mrs. Foster's lemonade. "Don't remind us."

"Sorry."

"It's all right." *Is it?* her conscience demanded. Juli just stared out the window.

Mom made the last turn before reaching the street where the Scotts and Rileys lived. "Why don't we leave the van at Shannon's and walk home? I'd like to stretch my legs. You're welcome to come with us, second daughter."

"Okay."

Juli tried to make up for sounding so grumpy. "It doesn't take you long to accept." She forced a laugh and was surprised at how much better she felt.

Mom chuckled. "You must be thinking of the Quaker story, Shannon."

Shannon shook her dark head and looked puzzled. "Quaker story?"

"Yes." Mom expertly guided the van into

the Riley driveway, shut off the motor, and turned toward Shannon. Her eyes danced with mischief. "An old story says a stranger dropped into a Quaker home just at supper time. His host asked him if he wanted to eat with them. The man said no, but when the Quaker's wife put the food on the table, it smelled so good the stranger said, 'I've changed my mind. I'll be glad to eat with you.' According to the story, the Quaker sternly looked at the man and said, 'Friend, thou hast refused once.' "

Shannon laughed. "From now on, I'll be afraid to say no for fear you won't let me change my mind!" She crawled out of the van.

"Bingo." Juli tumbled after her and stretched. "Ugh. My muscles are so stiff."

"Same here. Let me check to see if Dad's home. He was either going to catch a ride or come on the bus." She lightly ran to the beautifully carved front door. A few minutes later she returned wearing a frown. "Dad's at your place."

A quiver vibrated in Juli's stomach. "How come?"

"He didn't say." Shannon looked anxious. "He sounded fine, so there can't be anything wrong."

"I hope not." For an instant, Juli felt she was back at the farm telling Dave she didn't see how much more could go wrong today. Had she been mistaken?

"Everything looks quiet enough," Mom observed when they reached the Scott home. "Gary's here, but it's time he would be. One of the nice things about the desk job is that he usually has more regular hours."

"I hear Dad's laugh," Shannon commented when they reached the porch of the yellow house with its sparkling white shutters and flower boxes filled with rainbow blossoms.

Juli felt her knees sag. Nothing too terrible could be wrong if Dad and Sean Riley were laughing. She held the door for Mom and Shannon, but sent her voice ahead to announce their arrival. "We're home. Lucky you."

"Come in here, young lady. I want to talk to you," Dad called.

Juli shivered. What on earth! She hastily reviewed what she might have done to make Dad sound like a stern parent, especially when he had been laughing with Sean the moment before. Nothing came to mind. Had she failed to do something? Take out the garbage? Unload the dishwasher?

"I don't think so," she muttered, then reluctantly followed Shannon and Mom into the living room.

Not a trace of a smile lingered on Dad's face. Sean Riley appeared totally absorbed in reading a letter.

"All right, Juli. We know who did it." Gary Scott's eyes gleamed with an unreadable expression. "You may as well make it easy on yourself and confess."

Worn out from the horrible, wonderful, up-and-down day, Juli did what Christy had done a few hours earlier. She burst into tears.

Chapter 9

Silence fell over the Scotts' living room, so deep Juli's sobs sounded like explosions. The next instant, Dad cleared his chair in a mighty leap, and had her in his arms. "Juli, I am so sorry."

She grabbed a handful of his shirt and pressed it against her scorching face. From the shelter of his strong and protective arms, her childish action seemed incredible. How could she have lost control like that? Shame dried her tears. "I-I'm sorry. It's just . . ." She stopped. How could she explain that so much had happened, the slightest criticism cut deeply?

"Christy Gilmore either saw or thought she saw someone in the woods," Mom stated. "She said he spied on her from the bushes and looked at her as though he hated her. It upset all of us."

Juli started to say it wasn't just Christy. Shannon's troubled gaze stopped her. Further explanations would make her feel as bad as Juli. She pulled free from Dad's comforting hug. She accepted the wad of tissues Anne Scott held out, blew her nose, and felt better. "Thanks, Mom. Nothing like a good cry to clear the air." She braced herself. "Okay, Dad. What did I do?"

Guilt and regret spread all over Gary Scott's face. He sent an appealing glance toward Sean, who had risen and still held the letter he'd been reading when Juli came in. "You did nothing except be your own wonderful self," Dad said fiercely. "Listen to this." He practically snatched the letter from Sean and read in a choked voice that showed how terrible he felt for giving Juli a bad time:

"Dear Mr. Scott: Congratulations. We like your recently submitted story and plan to run it in a future issue. Enclosed please find our check for $250.00. We are purchasing First North American serial rights and —"

The roller coaster of emotions Juli had ridden all day sped up, up, up, carrying her from tears to triumph. "You sold it. They bought it. Oh, Dad!" She threw her arms around him. "Where's the check?"

"Here." He handed her a pink piece of paper. She held it against his chest and read the magic words on the tear-off stub: "First North American serial rights for 'Murder in Black and White.' "

Juli's voice rose to a screech. "Two hundred and fifty dollars! Fantastic."

"That's not all. The letter also says they would like to see other stories." Dad couldn't keep pride and excitement from his voice. "It's all your doing, Juli. That's what I meant when you came in. I grew discouraged and probably wouldn't have submitted the story again." He smiled, but still looked anxious. "Forgive me for making you cry?"

She raised her chin and blinked wet lashes. "If you'll forgive me for acting like a baby . . ." She cocked her head to one side. "On second thought, I think you should pay a fine for scaring me. Like taking us all out to dinner. Right, ladies and gentleman of the jury?" She looked at the others.

"Absolutely," Mom seconded.

Shannon nodded until her dark bangs hopped. "Just don't tell the boys how much we eat, after today's picnic dinner!"

"We won't." Sean laughed and patted his stomach.

"Sentence accepted. I can't think of a better way to spend some of my prize money," Dad agreed. "For tonight only, the sky's the limit. Everyone get into their best clothes."

The Rileys promptly excused themselves and went out. Mom headed for the shower.

Dad laid a restraining hand on his daughter's arm. "Wait, please, Juli." Happiness over the story sale fled and concern darkened his gray eyes. "Are you really all right? You've had some pretty traumatic things happen in the last couple of years. What about this Christy thing? Did she really see a man?"

"We don't know," Juli reluctantly admitted. "Nothing looked out of the ordinary when the men and boys investigated. On the other hand, Dave says Christy never makes up stuff to get attention. Their family is like ours — everyone is appreciated." She hesitated, then whispered, "I don't want to worry Mom, but do you think the person who wrote that note to me and the man Shannon calls 'Christy's spy' are the same person?"

"Not likely." He kissed her cheek. "To be on the safe side, I'll alert the Paynes while you and your mother make yourselves even more beautiful than you already are. I showed them the note this morning then passed it on to the prosecuting attorney in the Brett Jones case."

"Thanks, Dad." A warm glow replaced fears. With him and the FBI on the job, she could relax and enjoy dinner.

Less than an hour later, the Scotts and Rileys were off for a special evening. "We have some good-looking women here, don't we?" Dad asked Sean.

Shannon blushed until her cheeks matched her thin, pink cotton dress. Mom's blue eyes glowed above her sapphire-blue sheer print. Juli straightened her shoulders and pretended to pick an imaginary thread off her new soft-green cotton. "It's fun to dress up after wearing jeans and shorts so much," she announced. "A shower and clean clothes do wonders for the morale."

"So does being taken to the best place in Bellingham," Shannon whispered when they arrived at the destination Dad had chosen. "Mercy me, I must have a hollow foot. I'm hungry again."

"You mean hollow leg," Juli whispered back. The atmosphere around them didn't encourage her usual reaction to a Rileyism. Heavy silver on rich white tablecloths, sparkling crystal, fine china, and fresh flowers on each table spelled elegance with a capital E.

Dad, Mom, and Sean kept things light and interesting during the excellent dinner. Juli suspected they had agreed to avoid anything unpleasant and determined to do the same. She felt her lips curve into a smile. Several months ago she'd found her mind wandering during church. Upsetting events from all the yesterdays hammered at her brain. So did wondering what her tomorrows might bring. She had squeezed her eyes shut and prayed for God to help her forget the "before and after," so she could appreciate her now. Tonight was another good time to simply enjoy.

A few hours later, Juli patted Clue, reached for her journal, and wrote:

Lord, did you ever see such a day? Talk about peaks and valleys, and not just scenery. Mrs. Sorenson calls story obstacles and temporary victories peaks and valleys. If I were doing an outline, I'd have plenty of both!

She listed them in order, putting a fat, black bullet next to each.

- *Waking up to a perfect day*
- *Dad finding the JULIE death threat note.*
- *Seeing the excited faces of our adopted grandparents.*
- *The drive to the Fosters.*
- *Their warm greetings for the Destination Birdsview caravan.*
- *The peaceful valley walled in by forest and mountains.*

116

- *The feeling nothing bad could ever find me there.*
- *The great picnic, singing, and stories from the olden days.*
- *Christy and her spy, and wondering if I'd been followed.*
- *My shattered peace and being angry at creeps who spoil things.*
- *My talk with Dave.*
- *Mr. Foster's beautiful prayer. It was like a blessing.*
- *Praying for strength to not ruin the day for our guests.*
- *Seeing and hearing their appreciation.*
- *Coming home and misunderstanding Dad's teasing.*
- *Dad's special hug that said better than words how sorry he was.*
- *Learning his story sold.*
- *The great time we had going out with Shannon and her father.*

Juli waited for a long time, then put down her journal and pencil. "Thanks, Lord, for being there for me, no matter what. I'd never make it without You." She yawned and turned out her light. Yet something nagged at her, a piece of unfinished business she needed to remember and settle before falling asleep. She mentally ran over the day again and stopped when she remembered how she'd cried and buried her face against Dad's shirt. Something about the moment haunted her — something harder to catch and hold than a hummingbird.

She concentrated, trying to relive the feeling. "That's it," she said into her pillow. "I realized I can't handle criticism right now." She stared into the darkness and automatically reached for Clue. His soft fur felt comforting against her cheek. "Is that why I keep putting off writing, except in my journal?" she asked him. "After all I said to Dad about not giving up, am I afraid if I send a story out and it gets rejected, I won't be able to stand it?"

She squeezed her stuffed bear. "That could be why every time I think about working on my Christmas story, I find some excuse not to write. It isn't writer's block or even laziness. It's just plain being scared 'More Than Tinsel' will be turned down. Funny. Just saying it out loud makes me feel better."

Juli's mind drifted to the story idea she had started planning months earlier. Excitement flowed through her. She flipped her light back on and padded to her desk, bare feet moving noiselessly on the soft carpet. Too bad she couldn't sneak to the den and use the computer. She shook her head. Even if she couldn't sleep, Dad and Mom needed their rest. She'd make do with her notes and what she had printed out to show her Honors writing teacher.

Back in bed, she punched her pillows, squirmed into a comfortable position, and began to read. She nodded at her basic plot: a family who decorates their home for Christmas but holds so much bitterness in their hearts there is no room for joy. Her one-sentence theme was good, too: "It takes more than tinsel to make a happy Christmas."

The old joy of writing came back with a rush when she read the brief plot description Mrs. Sorenson had praised highly.

"Sixteen-year-old Wendy Thompson spends hours decorating her home for Christmas. Yet all the holly wreaths and candles, bright lights and presents can't erase bitter memories or the anger between her brother and her parents.

"Wendy knows it will take more than tinsel to bring peace and joy to the Thompson home this holiday season. How can she bring the real meaning of Christmas into a house where no one else seems to care?"

Juli yawned. Even her newly awakened desire to write couldn't compete with the hours of fresh air and hiking, emotional strain, and excitement over Dad's story sale. She turned out her light for the second time and fell asleep almost before her hand left the switch.

Juli awoke to gray, weeping skies. After breakfast, Mom suggested they invite Shannon over and take advantage of the cool day to fill the cookie jar. By noon, the fat pottery jar held enough sugar and molasses cookies to "feed an army or last this family two days," according to Mom. "That husband of mine."

"Mmm." Shannon mumbled through an enormous mouthful of warm molasses cookie. "My tooth is sweet, too."

Juli stared at her. "You mean you have a sweet tooth."

"Whatever." Shannon grinned and sipped orange spice herbal tea. "Mom, can you spare another cookie for a poor, starving immigrant?"

Juli choked on her own tea. "Wrong on all three counts. You aren't poor. No one is starving who eats as many cookies as you have. You stopped being an immigrant a long time ago. I know you aren't a citizen yet, but you will be." She stared at her friend. "Your grandfather and father are citizens, aren't they? I never thought to ask. I guess I just took it for granted."

The dark head with its thick bangs bobbed up and down. Shannon fell into the brogue that added tang to her speech when she felt things deeply. "For certain, and I'm a someday-citizen. Dad and Grand became naturalized shortly after they came to Washington. They said one of the proudest moments of their lives was when they were for bein' sworn in on your Fourth of July, along with many, many others. America has been good to them. They're glad to officially be part of it."

She hesitated, and the blue-gray eyes behind her long fringe of lashes looked solemn. "I love Ireland. It's the home of my ancestors. I also love the country that's adopted my family and me. I can hardly wait to be eighteen and apply for naturalization. A few months after, I'll be scheduled for my tests." She grinned. "Niver in me life have I studied the likes of how I'll study then!"

Mom smiled at her. "I'd say that's worth another cookie." She passed the almost empty plate. A gleam of sunlight came through the window. "Good. The storm's moved on. It's gorgeous outside."

Juli looked out the window. Raindrops sparkled on grass and flowers, making their brilliant colors more dazzling than ever. The world had a fresh-washed look. "It sure is. The sun will dry the park tennis courts. Who's for a game?"

Mom held her hand up like a little girl. "I am, if my daughter and adopted daughter will help clean up the kitchen."

"Sure thing. Better watch out, Mom. Shannon has a wicked serve. Don't forget a headband. It's already warming up." Juli tackled the sticky cookie bowl and utensils while her someday-citizen friend brushed flour off the breadboard and washed the rolling pin.

The spur-of-the-moment tennis tournament proved a smash success. Literally. Mom defeated Juli. Juli bested Shannon by a narrow margin. Mom and Shannon seesawed the entire game until Shannon smashed a ball just inside the sideline. Mom lunged for it and missed, giving her opponent the winning point.

"We're pretty evenly matched." Mom dropped to the grass beside the court where Juli had impartially cheered both her and Shannon on.

Shannon pulled off her headband and mopped at her sweaty face. "Mercy me, you kept me running all over the place! You must play a lot."

"Actually I don't." Mom laughed. In her sleeveless white blouse and modest-length shorts, she looked almost as young as her daughter. "I surprised myself. Not bad for an old lady, huh?"

"Old lady!" Shannon's contagious laugh rang out clear and happy. "Can't you just see it, Juli? Headlines in the paper twenty years from now will scream WHITE-HAIRED GRANDMOTHER BEATS THE TENNIS SHOES OFF OPPONENTS." She flopped to the ground and grinned at them.

Juli laughed until her sides hurt. "Excuse me? You don't beat tennis shoes off an opponent. You beat their socks off."

"Details, details. What if they aren't wearing socks?" Shannon flung her arms over her head and stared at the sky.

Juli didn't bother to answer. She simply lay still and treasured the moments of fun and quiet. A deep sigh started up from her toes. She stopped it before it could slip out of her throat. Words couldn't adequately express how she felt. Her appreciation for the togetherness in the middle of a world gone crazy went far too deep for anything but her memory. Someday when she needed a scene for a story it would be waiting. She'd pull it from the storage compartment of her brain, just like she pulled up material stored on the computer hard drive.

Juli raised one arm to shade her eyes from the sun and her stomach grumbled loudly. "I hate to admit it, but I'm hungry again."

"Why am I not surprised?" Anne Scott sat up and gently brushed a ladybug from her bare arm. She glanced at her watch. "Time to go home, anyway. Thanks for including me. It's been fun."

"Anytime," Juli told her. "Not a lot of mothers are that good at tennis."

Shannon's eyes twinkled and she lazily got up. "Or baking cookies."

"Flattery will get you everywhere, so keep talking," Mom said. All three laughed and headed across the park and down the sidewalk toward home.

Chapter 10

It didn't take Mom, Juli, and Shannon long to walk the short, tree-shaded distance between the park and home. When they were within a block of the house, the wail of sirens split apart the neighborhood calm. Two police cars passed them and stopped just ahead. Officers spilled out. "They aren't — they can't be going to our home. Uh-oh. They are." Juli turned a frightened gaze toward Mom and started to run.

"Good grief. What now?" Anne Scott and Shannon took out after her.

What now? What now? What now? Juli's thudding feet kept time to the words. She reached the front yard and started to race up the walk. A faint acrid odor hung in the air. Was her house on fire?

"Hold it!" A uniformed police officer barred her way.

"We live here," Juli protested.

"It doesn't make any difference." The officer's level gaze turned from her to Mom. "No one goes near the house until we finish checking it out."

"Why?" Juli demanded. "What's wrong?"

"Nothing, we hope, but we aren't taking chances." Thin lips sealed tighter than an oyster shell. "Just stay back, will you?"

Mom came out of her shock enough to plead, "Will you notify my husband, please? Gary Scott, Washington State Police." She gave the number and extension where he could be reached.

"Will do. WSP. That may explain it."

Juli grabbed his sleeve. "Explain what?"

He shook her off, gave her a withering look, and didn't answer.

"What's going on here?" a stern voice demanded from behind them.

Juli whirled. "Andrew!" She had never been happier to see anyone. "What are you doing here?"

"It isn't important." Andrew Payne spoke to the officer, too low for Juli's listening ears to make out what he said.

Recognition and something else came across the officer's face — an unspoken acknowledgment the new arrival was now in charge. "Yes, sir," he said. He glanced at the others. "Someone called and said they heard an explosion at this address. We were here in five minutes."

"Explosion!" Mom's fingers dug into Juli's bare arm.

126

The officer apologetically shook his head. "Sorry. That's all we know. Everything looks fine from here," he added hopefully.

Juli looked from him to the house. An across-the-street neighbor stood halfway between her and the house. Without waiting to ask permission, she ran toward him. Andrew and the others followed close behind.

A powerful arm stopped and held her. "Let me handle this," Andrew hissed. When she nodded, he asked the man who stood staring at the backyard, "Are you the person who called in?"

"Yes. It's just like I reported on the phone," the excited man said. "I heard a bang, so loud it rattled windows. I thought maybe the furnace had blown, so I came over as soon as I called. Everything seemed fine, except the air smelled like gunpowder." He sniffed. "Most of it is gone now."

Three officers rounded the side of the house from the backyard. One of them held a paper bag. Juli's nerves jumped. Dad had taught her long ago that contrary to popular opinion, evidence is never put into plastic bags. Plastic sweats. Prints on the article can be damaged.

"What did you find?" Andrew barked.

"The remains of a highly illegal, heavy-duty piece of fireworks."

Mom's shoulders slumped in obvious relief. A moment later Gary Scott charged toward them from behind the parked police cars. "Is everyone all right?"

Why didn't he seem surprised there had been an explosion? Chills played tag up and down Juli's spine. He must be taking the JULIE note a whole lot more seriously than he let on. She caught his exchange of glances with Andrew Payne and her busy mind rushed on. Was that why Andrew just happened to be close enough to reach the Scott home within minutes after the police officers arrived? And why he had told her it wasn't important for her to know why he was there?

"Is it all right if we go inside?" Mom asked in a tired voice.

"We'll go first," Andrew told her. "Do you have the keys?"

She fumbled in her purse, pulled out her keys, and handed them to him.

Fifteen minutes later, the house received a clean bill of health and an all clear for the family, plus Shannon and Andrew, to enter. They gathered in the quiet living room.

Shannon spoke for the first time since they came home from the park. "There's something funny going on. You'd have to actually be in the backyard to set off that kind of fireworks." Her eyes looked enormous. "Mercy me, no one could even throw a firecracker that far, not from any direction!"

"We know," Andrew spit out. "It will be interesting to see if our piece of evidence turns up anything."

"Why would anyone be for sneaking into the yard and setting off fireworks bound to attract attention?" she persisted.

"Intimidation." The ugly word hung in the air just as the acrid stench left by the explosion had earlier.

Shannon gasped. She looked like someone had run into her at full speed. Gary Scott exchanged another glance with Andrew. Juli saw the FBI man nod, then Dad said, "We didn't want to worry you, Shannon, but Juli received a rather unpleasant note yesterday morning. We hoped it might be a crank thing. Evidently it isn't. Someone doesn't want her to testify at Brett Jones's trial, and is going to a lot of trouble to frighten her out of doing so."

The muscles of Shannon's throat contracted. She wordlessly stared at Dad and slid down into her chair until she looked small and defenseless.

Juli felt sorry for her friend. It was bad enough to be harassed by some creep without Shannon having to worry about it. "At least it wasn't something that would actually hurt us," she pointed out in a weak voice.

Andrew Payne refused to rationalize. "Not yet." He hoisted himself from his chair. His red hair stood on end where he'd raked his fingers through it. "I advise you two and your friends to be careful. Very careful. Gary told me about Christy's spy. It may mean nothing, or a lot. We don't know who or what we're dealing with here."

"Do you think it's Brett?" Shannon asked in a hollow-sounding voice. "It just isn't fair. We didn't see a thing that awful Wednesday!"

"Jones is in no condition to accept that," Andrew reminded. "We don't know at this time, but it may not even be Brett. It doesn't make sense for him to risk being picked up on a minor charge when he's out on bail." He patted Shannon's arm and his face softened. "I don't want to scare you. I just want you to be aware there are a lot of crazies out there. It takes time for us to catch them and put them away." He and Dad headed for the hall and front door, leaving Mom and the girls silently staring after them.

"I should go home." Shannon looked fearfully at the door.

"I'll walk with you." Juli hopped to her feet.

Dad's amused voice came from the doorway. "It looks to me like you two need showers," he teased Mom and Juli. "How about my walking the pretty colleen home?"

Color rushed to Shannon's smooth cheeks and she gave Dad a grateful glance. "Thanks. It's been quite a day." She smiled at Mom and Juli, but it didn't hide her fears.

"Just when she got over being afraid to testify, this has to happen," Juli complained after Dad left with Shannon.

"I know. The whole thing has left me feeling like a rag doll, and I'm only indirectly involved in the trial," Mom confessed. She gave Juli a weary smile. "One thing about life in our family: It's never dull! I can hardly believe that less than twenty-four hours ago we were laughing and celebrating your father's story being accepted." She bit her lip. "Sorry. A shower will restore my drooping spirits."

Juli watched Mom walk out, head up and chin high, then slowly went to her own room to clean up. As Mom had said, a shower could work wonders. She stood under the spray for a long time, wishing the soapy water washing away dust and perspiration would take fear as well. It did help. By the time she dressed in a soft yellow shorts outfit and blew her hair dry, she felt better.

Up and down. Up and down. Juli felt more on a roller coaster than ever a few hours later when she received a call from the local newspaper that had run her story about observing a trial. She burst into the living room shouting, "Guess what!" Her cheeks burned and her eyes glowed.

Dad grinned and Mom looked up from a magazine. "It must be good."

"It's wonderful! There's been quite a bit of reader response to my article," Juli proudly told them. She dropped to the rug and sat cross-legged. "So much so the paper is going to do something it's never done before."

"And that would be . . ." Dad prompted.

"Even though the paper has occasionally used items written by young adults, they've never had a young person consistently writing about things from her perspective." She clasped her hands and felt a broad grin stretch across her face. "The publisher is announcing a writing contest in tomorrow's paper. The winner, who has to be a sophomore or junior in a Bellingham school, will have her very own column! That's so she can do it for at least two years, in case she attends college elsewhere after she graduates. Isn't that fantastic?"

Dad chuckled. "The winner doesn't have to be a *she*, as you so confidently predict. There's at least a remote possibility it will be a *he*."

"In your dreams," Juli smirked. "Think I'm going to let a guy beat me out of winning? I'd give anything to be the new columnist." She hastily amended, "I mean I really want to win and will try hard. Excuse me, please. I have to call Shannon and see if she wants to enter." She started toward the door, feeling torn. "Part of me hopes she won't. It will cut down on the competition a lot, because she's such a good writer. Another part knows it could give her something to concentrate on besides the trial."

"You're right about that," Anne Scott quietly said. "It hurt me to see the expression on her face when she learned about the note." She left her chair and crossed to Juli. "I understand what you're saying. Shannon and your dad have both sold stories. You'd like to win, not so much for the money, but to prove to yourself you can do it, and have the opportunity to be read. It's okay to feel that way, Juli. Your concern for Shannon shows you're willing to accept whatever happens is right. With such an attitude, you'll be fine."

Her mother's praise settled into Juli's heart like a warm mitten on a cold day. She ran to call her friend. A few minutes later she came back giggling and said Shannon didn't think she'd enter the contest. "She also warned me not to count my columns before they're written. When I told her she meant not to count my chickens before they were hatched, she laughed and wanted to know when we started keeping chickens!"

The next afternoon, the girls went shopping downtown. Sparkling windows held large SALE signs, promising everything from 10 percent to 50 percent off. Both Juli and Shannon loved good clothes, but neither could spend a fortune. Instead, they looked for the 40 percent and 50 percent off the last marked clearance price sales at the nicer stores in Bellingham. They seldom came home empty-handed, and gloated over the bargains. Why pay a hundred dollars, "which we wouldn't," Shannon reminded, when they could often purchase the same thing for much less?

"So what kind of competition do you think you'll have in the contest?" Shannon asked, twirling a rack of jeans to find her size.

"Not counting you?"

"Not counting me. I decided for sure not to enter. Aren't you glad?"

"You bet I am," Juli frankly told her. "How are these colors on me?" She held up a printed blouse and craned her neck to look over Shannon's head at a mirror.

"Okay, but not great. These are better."

Shannon offered a different blouse. "You haven't answered my question."

"Uh, right. I don't know who might enter from the other schools, except Ashley Peterson." She made a face and raised her voice so she could be heard over the babble from a crowd of high school girls also looking for bargains. "She'll be first in line. You weren't here freshman year, when I went to Cove."

"Is she good?"

"Yeah." Juli knew she sounded glum. "That's not the worst of it. Every time she pulled an A, the teacher praised her writing. Ashley put on an affected smile then said, 'Oh, thank you, Mrs. Daniels. I didn't think it was all that good.' I'm glad she didn't get transferred to Hillcrest. If she wins, no one will be able to live with her for the next two years."

"Is she the girl who walked right past us without speaking when Hillcrest played Cove in basketball?"

"She's the one. I shouldn't get steamed up, I guess. If she wins, she wins."

Shannon looked troubled. "I know she acted unfriendly, but I felt kind of sorry for her. Her clothes were clean, but not really —"

An icy voice cut in from behind them. "Save your feeling sorry for someone who needs it. I don't."

Juli and Shannon whipped around to face the subject of their conversation, complete with brightly flushed cheeks and sneering lips. Of all the rotten coincidences! What chance was there Ashley Peterson would be at the sale table next to theirs at the exact moment they were discussing her? The nagging knowledge she shouldn't have been putting another girl down no matter what made Juli feel slightly sick. So did the hurt that even anger couldn't completely hide in the pale blue eyes.

"I-I'm sorry." Shannon looked miserable.

"You should be." Ashley shot her a deadly look then turned to Juli. "You're worse. Everyone used to say what a great Christian you were. Some Christian, talking about people behind their backs." She gritted her teeth and added, "I may not have money and a lot of cute clothes, but at least I'm not a hypocrite. I don't pretend to be all religious and goody-goody, when I'm really mean and gossipy." She turned, her long brown hair flying, then looked back over her shoulder.

"When I win the newspaper contest and become a columnist, you'll be sorry." Her childish threat echoed in Juli's ears long after Ashley ran out of the store.

Chapter 11

"Ashley, wait!" Juli started after the girl whose bitter words had cut deep.

Shannon grabbed Juli's arm. "Let her go. She's hurt and angry." Misery clouded her eyes. "She has every right to be. Ashley didn't sneak up and eavesdrop. She couldn't help hearing. We also both know better than to talk about people, and not just in a crowded store." She sighed. "There goes any chance of inviting her to our church youth group, if we ever had one."

"I know." All the joy of shopping with Shannon left Juli. She looked at the neat racks of clothing that had appeared so attractive a few minutes earlier. "Do you want any of these clothes?"

"No. Every time I wore them, I'd remember the awful feeling I have right now." Shannon put back the blouse she had been holding up for Juli's inspection. "Let's go home. Shopping isn't fun anymore."

The girls remained quiet on the bus ride home. Their friendly driver's words, "Good to see you both. Like I say, one without the other is . . ." and their chorus ". . . like ham without eggs," produced only half-smiles at the worn-out cliché with which the driver, Fred Halvorsen, always greeted them.

"Want to come home with me?" Juli asked when they reached the bus stop halfway between the Scott and Riley homes.

"Yes. No. I don't know. I can't stop thinking about Ashley."

"Neither can I." Julie stared at a dandelion poking its shaggy yellow head up through a crack in the pavement. "Let's go tell Mom. Maybe we'll feel better."

Shannon brightened up right away. "Good idea."

Ten minutes later the three sat in the quiet backyard sipping icy lemonade. "You can't know how awful we felt when we realized Ashley had been standing there listening to the whole conversation," Shannon said. "It's not like she could have walked away or thought we were talking about someone else."

"Would it have made it any more right if she had?" Anne Scott quietly asked.

"No." Juli traced designs on her frosty glass and refused to look at Mom. "I've heard Ashley say *worse* things about people, though."

"I don't remember hearing you say she ever pretended to be a Christian," Mom crisply reminded. "We can't expect non-Christians to live as followers of Jesus are supposed to."

Juli sagged like a pricked balloon. "Meaning us. None of this is Shannon's fault. I'm the one who mimicked Ashley. All Shannon said was that she felt sorry for Ashley, and —"

"Which to a sensitive girl is as bad as other criticism," Mom pointed out.

"Yeah. What should we do?"

Mom turned her lemonade glass round and round. "What do you think?"

Juli felt more guilty than ever. It made her mumble, "Why can't you just tell me what to do, like when I was a little kid? It was so much easier."

"That's why." Mom's level voice brought Juli's gaze to her unsmiling face. "You aren't a little kid. You're sixteen years old and smart enough to know Dad and I won't always be around to tell you what to do. In a few years you're going to be making major life choices and decisions. The more responsibility you take for your actions now, the better you'll be prepared to face a confusing world. It won't be easy. It never is. It *is* part of growing up."

She leaned her head back on the chaise lounge. "I remember only too well when I was your and Shannon's age." A rueful smile tilted her lips. "One minute I acted like a child, the next, a young woman! Why? Because that's how I felt. Part of me clung to the habit of having my parents call the shots like a coach at a ball game. Another part fluttered wings of independence." She made a face. "End of story number 462. Or is it 597?"

"I love your little stories," Shannon told her. She swirled the small amount of lemonade left in her glass and drank it before adding, "Mother and I used to talk like this. I miss it. Thanks so much for being my second mom."

Juli's throat tightened at the depth of feeling in her friend's voice. It had been bad enough when Dad was missing. She couldn't imagine not having Mom, even though they didn't always agree. One good thing: She'd been taught long ago the art of disagreeing without being disagreeable. Even the most serious discussions in the Scott household never became shouting matches. Now she gave Mom a big grin. "Right as usual, much as I hate to admit it. Besides, you turned out okay. Maybe we will, too, but it doesn't solve the problem of Ashley."

"No, it doesn't." Mom's matching grin tossed the problem right back in the girls' laps and challenged them to solve it.

Shannon reached for the lemonade pitcher and refilled her glass. "Why don't we write her a note and tell her we're really sorry?"

A bright idea flitted into Juli's mind. She instantly rejected it. Such a drastic action was too big a sacrifice for just gossiping. *Is it too big to repair Ashley's belief that being a Christian doesn't make a difference?* a small inside voice mocked. Juli squirmed, wanting to tell the little voice to keep still. She couldn't. Gathering her courage with both hands she said, "I could tell Ashley I've decided not to enter the newspaper contest." The idea grew like Pinocchio's nose when he lied. "It would show her I'm sorry for talking behind her back."

Stone-cold, dead silence greeted her announcement.

Juli rushed on, caught up in her plan to make things right. "I don't need the money. From the looks of Ashley's clothes, she does. Like Shannon started to say in the store today, they're clean, but not really in style — wrong length and colors. I hope I don't sound snobbish." She anxiously looked at the others.

"Thank goodness I only got as far as I did," Shannon put in.

"What do you think, Mom? Is this the right choice?"

Anne Scott looked thoughtful and didn't answer. Shannon tried to lighten things up. "It's actually a not-to-write choice, as in not enter the contest."

Juli ignored her and watched Mom's gaze follow a monarch butterfly from blossom to blossom. "What are you thinking?" she finally asked.

Anne turned toward her. "I was putting myself in Ashley's place."

"And?" Juli held her breath and waited.

"Speaking for Ashley, I'd say it's the worst thing that could happen."

Juli stared at her. "Y-you would? Why?"

Mom sat up straight. "Okay. I'm hurt and angry. Most of all, I'm humiliated. I receive a phone call or letter from the person chiefly responsible for my feeling that way. If I don't hang up or tear up the message without reading it, I discover she isn't going to try for the contest. I already know how much it means to her. She made her ambitions clear when we competed in junior high."

"How do you feel now?" Shannon asked. "I mean, as Ashley?"

"Absolutely furious! How dare Juli Scott

patronize me? She has some nerve to assume that if she enters the contest, she'll automatically win."

"I don't feel that way," Juli protested. "I know I may not win."

"As Ashley, I'm convinced you do," Mom told her. "What fun is there in winning when another girl is playing martyr and bragging she could have been the young adult columnist?" She paused a moment to let it sink in.

"What if my clothes aren't the latest? Why does Juli think I've been baby-sitting all summer, if not to buy some that are? What do she and Shannon think I was doing at the sale, preparing to do some high-class shoplifting? There may be a dozen reasons I can't have all the cool clothes I want. Maybe Dad's out of work. Mom may be a single parent. I could have a little brother who has been so sick, most of our money goes for medical bills. Or maybe it's alcoholic parents.

"So along comes Goody Two-shoes prancing around doing her good deed for the day. Count me out. I may not have much else, but I have my pride. Juli Scott and that Irish friend of hers can't take that away from me. If I'm not a good enough writer to win the contest on my own and without a handicap, forget it!"

Juli had never felt lower in her life. "I-I . . . Mom, I'm so ashamed! Do you think all that stuff you said is true?"

"We can't know, honey. The Petersons may have a wonderful home life." Mom looked troubled. Her eyes darkened to light navy. "I can only tell you how I'd feel if I were Ashley and you told me you weren't entering the contest, especially after what happened in the store. You have to decide for yourself, but be sure to recognize there's a lot more at risk here than your desire to make up for what you did and said today."

"If my other foot was in the shoe, I'd feel that way, too," Shannon sighed. "It doesn't seem like enough, but maybe my idea of writing her an apology is best."

Still shaken by Mom's role-playing, Juli didn't tell her friend the expression was actually "shoe on the other foot."

"It makes a big difference when you stop to think there's a reason behind the way people act," Juli soberly said. "Ditto for how they feel. I'm with Shannon. The last thing I'd need if I were Ashley Peterson is for Juli Scott to make me feel like a loser even if I win."

Shannon reluctantly stood. "I need to get home, but let's write our apology first. Neither of us will feel better until we do."

They headed for the den and wasted a dozen sheets of Juli's best notepaper before they settled on a two-sentence message.

Dear Ashley,
We are really sorry for the way we acted. You have every right to be angry, but we hope you will forgive us.

"It sounds cold," Juli complained. "Should we add, 'good luck in the contest'?"

Shannon shook her head violently. "Mercy me, no! Leave it the way it is."

Juli looked up the Petersons' address in the phone book and copied it on an envelope. "Okay. We'll show Mom our note and I'll walk you halfway home."

Once Anne Scott gave her approval of the apology, the cloud of regret lifted a bit. As Shannon misquoted on the way down the path to the sidewalk, "No sense crying over milk that's been spilled."

"You mean spilt milk."

Shannon looked innocent. "Isn't that what I said?"

"Well, sort of." Juli laughed at her friend's expression. "Anyway, you're right. We admitted we were wrong and wrote our note to apologize." She walked a few steps. "I can tell you one thing. I won't forget how rotten

I felt when Mom pretended to be Ashley. I hope it helps me not be so quick to judge."

"So do I — both of us, I mean," Shannon quickly agreed. "Are you sure you don't want to walk all the way home with me?"

Juli started to say no, but something in Shannon's voice stopped her. She checked her watch. "Sure. Since we cut our shopping trip short, I'll still have time to help Mom fix dinner." They lazily strolled the few blocks to the Riley home, discussing everything from the next youth group activity to how fast the summer months were passing.

The phone was ringing when Shannon unlocked the front door. "Pick the mail up off the floor while I answer, okay?" She dashed down the hall.

"Sure." Juli grabbed the letters and magazines and carried them to the living room. She put them on a table and sat down in a chair, her legs straight out in front of her. A few minutes later Shannon came back wearing a disgusted look.

"I get so tired of calls telling me about specials on windshield replacements or offering to clean our rugs. What's in the mail?"

"Really, Miss Riley. Are you unaware tampering with others' mail is a federal offense?" Juli said in a fair imitation of the judge in the case they had seen tried. "As well as showing vulgar curiosity," she added in her own voice.

Shannon laughed and took the stack of mail to a chair near Juli. She riffled through it. "Bill. Bill. Advertisement. Letter for Dad." She broke off abruptly. "What's this on the bottom?" She held up an envelope and asked in a strangled voice, "Juli, did your threatening note just have your first name typed on it?"

"Yes. Misspelled." The full impact hit Juli a second later. She leaped from her chair, flew to Shannon, and knelt by her chair. "Did you get one, too?"

"I think so. It only has my first name." Shannon stared at the envelope as if it were a poisonous snake. "You open it. I can't." She pushed it into Juli's hands.

A quick slit of the envelope with a fingernail showed a single sheet of paper. Boldface type Juli knew without checking was Word for Windows Impact warned: DON'T TESTIFY AGAINST BRETT JONES. The skull and crossbones symbol from Wingdings followed.

Sweat crawled up Juli's spine. "It looks identical to mine, except your name is spelled right." She and Shannon examined the ugly message. "Mine was also taped to our front door. Someone must have shoved this into your mail slot. It couldn't have come in the mail." Juli got up. "We have to call Dad right away. He will contact Andrew. We'll call your father, too." She started for the phone.

Shannon sprang from her chair and followed. "I-I'm so upset I don't think anyone will be able to understand me. Will you make the calls, please?"

"I'll be glad to." Rage at a creep who could make the friend she loved so much look stricken and scared steadied Juli's shaking voice. "If Brett Jones thinks he can intimidate us, he can think again! No way is he going to get away with this kind of stuff."

"Do you really think it's Brett?" Shannon wanted to know.

Juli viciously punched in numbers and said while waiting for her call to go through, "Who else could it be?" She didn't want to alarm Shannon by suggesting worse possibilities. Besides, no big-time crime syndicate would be sending threatening notes. They'd take far more drastic measures to ensure Brett Jones didn't identify them.

Her hands went clammy at the thought. She tightened her hold on the phone. When Dad came on the line, she told him about

148

the letter. "It looks exactly like mine," she reported.

"Word for Windows Impact Wingdings?"

"Yes." Juli didn't elaborate.

"Was the threat under or on top of everything else?" Gary Scott demanded.

"Underneath. The very bottom piece."

"That gives us a clue as to time. Okay, Juli. Do exactly as I tell you. Call Mom and have her come get you in the car. Take Shannon to our place. Make sure she brings the letter, but keep it out of sight. When you go out the door, laugh and act natural. I know it's a tough assignment, but it could be necessary."

Juli's mouth felt dryer than the Sahara Desert in midsummer. "You think someone may be watching the house?"

"I hope not, but we won't take chances. Just do what I say. Now."

Chapter 12

By the end of the week, Juli and Shannon weren't alone when it came to death-threat letters. Each of their friends who had been at the Pizza Palace the Wednesday of the Chuckanut Community Bank robbery received one. Ted and Amy Hilton found theirs tucked under a windshield wiper of Amy's Mustang. Molly Bowen and John Foster's turned up on top of their mail. Dave Gilmore's was taped to the outside of his bedroom window.

All but Dave's were identical and appeared to have been made by the same computer. The terrifying difference in his letter was a thirteen-word postscript just below the skull and crossbones: IT PAYS TO WATCH OUT FOR YOUR FAMILY. SEE THAT YOU REMEMBER IT.

With the increased number of threats, the need for secrecy about them decreased. Andrew Payne asked Gary Scott to invite all those who received letters, and their parents, to meet at the Scott home the following night. "We'll be questioning neighbors to see if they noticed anything unusual," he added.

A sober-faced bunch of people gathered in the Scotts' backyard. Andrew Payne took charge. Juli sat on a blanket on the grass with Dave on one side, Shannon on the other. Thinking of the postscript on Dave's letter made Juli absolutely sick. The shocked faces of the others reflected her feelings.

Andrew Payne examined the notes closely, Dave's in particular. "Interesting."

Juli knew better than to ask why. She concentrated on the postscript. What could be more obvious? The sender of the note must either be Christy's spy, or at least know Dave had a little sister. Andrew's expression gave away nothing, yet Juli felt there had to be more to the cryptic message than what was on the surface. She was vaguely aware of Andrew telling the group he'd called them together to share anything that might have a bearing on the case, no matter how small. She barely heard him. Something she had told Mom earlier teased at her brain.

At last Juli remembered what she had said and when. It was after Mom role-played Ashley Peterson. Julie could hear herself saying, "It makes a big difference when you stop to think there's a reason behind the way people act." She felt she'd been given a key to a padlocked room. Suppose she pretended to put herself inside the letter writer's skin. Would seeing from that perspective unlock a padlocked door and help solve the mystery?

Something stirred within her. Remembering Andrew's warning, she tried to put on a poker face. Her mind ran from track to track at full speed. A dozen ideas clamored for attention. She dismissed most and concentrated on the one that persistently refused to be banished. What if the postscript on Dave's letter held not only a threat, but a clue? Juli tingled with excitement. Suppose the underlying message wasn't in the second sentence, but the first: IT PAYS TO WATCH OUT FOR YOUR FAMILY?

Juli felt she had just grabbed a raging lion by the tail. What if Brett Jones wasn't sending the death threats after all? What if a family member or close friend was trying to protect him by preventing the youth group members from testifying? Brett had said he didn't have a family. So what? He'd lied about other things, such as claiming to be eighteen when he was actually in his twenties.

Unable to hold her suspicions in for one minute longer, Juli fixed her gaze on Andrew and stared. She'd heard somewhere if you concentrated hard enough, a person would turn and look at you. It might not be true, but she couldn't think of another way to attract his attention without alerting the others in the room.

Andrew didn't budge, but Mary happened to glance Juli's way. Juli made her eyes as appealing as possible. The FBI agent evidently got her message, although for a few agonizing moments Juli wondered if she'd really seen a flash of response in Mary's face. Then the attractive woman stood and started toward the house. "I believe I'll get a drink of water," she said when some of the others looked up. "Juli, show me where the glasses are, will you?" She laughed easily. "I have a horror of searching through cupboards without a warrant!"

Juli stood, hoping relief wouldn't buckle her knees. "Sure. Soft drinks, anyone? Lemonade? Iced tea? Stay put, people. Dad will help me bring them."

"Peanuts, popcorn, lemonade . . ." Dave Gilmore sounded like a circus barker. "Sure you don't need more help, Juli? I'm your man." He gave her a meaningful look that normally would make her heart skip a beat.

Instead, Juli nearly panicked. Even though the other half of Scott and Gilmore, P.I.s, knew how to keep his mouth shut, she couldn't tell him her suspicions. At least not until after she shared them with Mary. "Thanks, but Dad needs the exercise, now that he has a desk job."

"Yeah. We can't have him getting soft." Dave grinned and settled back in his place on the blanket.

Juli smiled and opened the door for Mary. Dad followed close behind. "Cover for me," she whispered. "I have to talk with Mary."

Instant understanding lighted his gray eyes. "Sure, but make it fast." He grinned. "I can only rattle ice trays and glasses for so long without having your mother come see what's holding me up."

Mary laughed and Juli led her down the hall to the sunny yellow bedroom where Clue patiently waited. She softly closed the door. "I just had an idea," she breathlessly said. "Maybe the letter writer is *related* to Brett. Could that stuff about how it pays to watch out for your family be a clue?"

To Juli's relief, Mary didn't write off the suggestion, but considered it seriously. "It might. Thanks, Juli." She gave the younger girl a friendly smile. "I've been so busy trying to decide whether there's a connection between this person and Christy's spy, I haven't focused much on that aspect yet. Good work, super sleuth. I believe I've heard your family and friends call you that."

Juli felt herself blush. Praise from an FBI agent, even one who had become a close acquaintance, meant a whole lot. "Thanks," she said. "Uh, I guess we should get back to the others. Don't forget your water."

"I won't." Mary sounded amused.

"Pretty dumb, me reminding you." Juli's hand flew to her burning face.

"Not at all." Mary slipped an arm around her shoulders, as if sensing Juli's embarrassment. "Anyone can forget small but important details. It never hurts to be reminded." She trailed Juli back to the kitchen and filled to the brim with ice water the glass Juli handed her. Dad took the tray of drinks.

"I know it's going to be especially hard now for some of you to testify," Andrew told the young people when everyone had drinks.

Shannon stared at him with dark-lashed eyes. The Irish brogue that colored her speech when she felt deeply sounded more pronounced than ever. "It's for bein' far more important that we do, isn't it? We can't just let a *spalpeen* — a rascally sort of person — run around scarin' people, especially children." Her face twisted. " 'Tis bad enough threatenin' those at the Pizza Palace." A single tear appeared. She angrily brushed it away. "Christy Gilmore never hurt anyone. Even though I don't know much, I'll not be for buttonin' my tongue!"

Stunned silence followed Shannon's personal declaration of independence, then a nervous giggle erupted from Juli. It triggered healing laughter that ran through the group like an electrical charge. Every person there knew the pretty Irish colleen's habit of misquoting, but this time she had outdone herself!

Shannon sighed. "Mercy me, what was I for sayin' wrong this time?"

"You either hold your tongue or button your lip," Juli told her between giggles. "You don't button your tongue." She laughed again.

"How about holding your lip?" John Foster teased.

"Back off or you'll be holding your lip," Ted Hilton warned, pretending to swing at his friend. John promptly ducked and grinned.

Andrew Payne's craggy smile made a different person of him. "Thanks, Shannon. We needed a good laugh. What about the rest of you?" His eyes twinkled. "Will you be for buttonin' your tongues?"

Shannon's statement inspired the rest of the Wednesday witnesses. "No." "Not me." "No way." Even Amy said, "We can't let someone push us around." Her chin raised, she added, "If we do, America will be no better than some of the countries in the world where people are afraid all of the time."

Juli sent the petite blond an amazed but approving smile. Had knowing Carlos Ramirez made the difference in Amy? It sounded like something he might say. Again she wondered how the cheerleader would handle peer pressure, if her friendship with their new classmate carried into their junior year.

"This is probably a dumb question," Shannon said hesitantly.

"The only dumb questions are those that don't get asked and won't be answered," Gary Scott told her.

"Thanks." She sent him a grateful smile. "I know it sounds crazy, but I just wondered if any of this could be related to Lord Leopold or Madame Zelda?"

"Absolutely not." Andrew's strong voice brought relief to Shannon's face. "They're still in Canada. We'll let our neighbors to the north take care of them."

He stood and stretched. "I appreciate your all coming, and we will stay in touch."

Mr. Gilmore, who had remained quiet during the meeting, asked, "Is it proper for me to ask if you have any leads?" He anxiously looked at his wife. "I'm more concerned over Christy than Dave. He's better able to take care of himself."

"No harm in asking," the FBI agent gruffly told him. "We do know some things that may be helpful." Andrew left it at that, but after the rest of the guests left, he turned to Juli. "What did you tell Mary?"

Dad grinned. "I was about to ask the same thing."

Juli repeated her suspicion. Andrew's smile made her add, "You already thought of the family connection, didn't you?" She gave an exaggerated sigh. "Either you or Mary are always a few steps ahead of me."

"Shouldn't we be?" he asked reasonably. "We've been at this a lot longer than you have. Think of yourself as an apprentice." He cocked his flaming red head to one side. "All things considered, you do all right."

"From anyone else, that would sound patronizing," Juli told him. "From you, I consider it a compliment."

"You should. Keep your eyes and ears open." He ushered Mary out.

The following afternoon, Juli and
Shannon decided to continue their interrupted shopping trip, only at the mall instead of downtown. "I hope we don't have
any encounters of the worst kind," Juli commented on the bus ride. Shannon and her
father still hadn't found a different car for
her. Sean Riley was so busy at the bank, he
had little time to think about anything else.

So much for Juli's wish. She and Shannon
had just stepped inside the mall doors when
a familiar voice called, "Hey, Juli. Shannon.
Wait up, will you?" Shannon's fingers dug
into Juli's arm. She barely felt the pain.
Speechless, she gazed into Brett Jones's
still-handsome face. It showed no signs of
strain or trouble. What looked like genuine
pleasure shone in his dark eyes.

"Fancy meeting you here." Brett flashed
his spectacular smile. "Shopping for school
clothes, I suppose. Guess I'll be missing
from the lunch bunch this fall."

Shannon gave a little squeak but Juli got
her voice back. "Why, Brett?"

"Why what?" He raised a dark eyebrow.
"Oh, why did I give that phony confession? I
guess I lost it for a while. It seemed the only
way I could get the cops off my back." He
looked straight into her blue eyes. "Are you

159

all still testifying? I really am innocent, you know."

Did his words hide a threat? "We've been subpoenaed. I don't know how many of us will be put on the stand." She bit her lip to keep from adding that none of them had seen anything. The least said about that, the better. Juli moved to one side so a plainly dressed woman carrying a large shopping bag could get past, but she returned her steady gaze to Brett.

"Sorry you are involved." He looked regretful and glanced at his watch. "I'm meeting someone but it's nice seeing you again. I really enjoyed hanging out with you. Tell Kareem and everyone hi. Oh. No hard feelings, okay?" He sauntered off without waiting for an answer.

Too stunned to answer, the girls watched him walk away.

"I wouldn't have believed it!" Shannon gasped.

"Neither would I." Juli's suspicions rose like foam on root beer. "He acted too cool to be real. How about forgetting shopping again and reporting to Dad?"

"We could follow Brett and see who he meets," Shannon hesitantly suggested.

Juli latched onto the idea eagerly. "Why not? Come on."

"Not you. Me." The woman who had elbowed past gave the girls a knowing look that identified her better than a badge or card. "I'll take over from here. Scram." Long strides carried the inconspicuously dressed woman down the mall.

"We need to get to Dad right away," Juli hissed in Shannon's ear. "Meeting Brett seems just too coincidental. Wonder if he followed us from home?" A bright idea hit her. "We could check the parking lot for a classic white Mustang."

"Why bother?" Shannon demanded. "That woman officer already knows he's here. It's Brett Jones who is being followed."

"I'd give my best story to know who he's meeting," Juli said. "It's disappointing to just be on the edge of things. Nancy Drew always ended up in the middle."

"She's a fictional heroine and we aren't," Shannon reminded. "Nancy Drew also made the local police look stupid part of the time. *I* think it's amazing people like your dad and the Paynes trust us enough to share what they do and let us be involved as much as we are. Even if it isn't enough to satisfy you."

"I know. Sorry I complained. Let's go see Dad."

A short time afterward, Juli was glad they

did. If they had disobeyed orders and followed Brett Jones, she and Shannon wouldn't have heard the latest news until later. Juli knew something had happened by the brusque way officers she'd known since childhood brushed her off. "Scott's too busy for personal visitors."

Curious to the breaking point, she and Shannon decided to wait. Dad actually came a few minutes later. He led them to his office. "I only have a minute, but you may as well know — it's already on TV. A one-man attempted bank robbery just took place in Mount Vernon." Worry lines in his face made him look old.

"It started like the others. Unfortunately, it didn't end that way. A bank teller panicked when she read the order to hand over the cash in her till. She froze and just stared at the waiting man. He fired two shots and fled, leaving behind screaming customers and a seriously wounded employee."

"Brett Jones wasn't involved," Juli whispered, feeling strangely glad. "Shannon and I just talked with him in the mall. I'm sure he wouldn't have had enough time to reach Mount Vernon by the time the robbery was committed."

"That's odd," Dad said. "The description of the robber tallies with Brett's."

Chapter 13

Gary Scott propped his elbows on his desk and leaned forward. "Juli, Shannon, are you absolutely positive Brett Jones couldn't get to Mount Vernon between the time of the attempted bank robbery and when you saw him?"

"Practically positive. We came straight here from there." Doubt crept into Shannon's eyes. "I suppose if he left immediately, he might have made it. On the other hand, if Brett planned to rob a bank miles away, why would he stand talking with us, then head down the mall like he had all the time in the world?"

Juli quickly put in, "He also must have been parked at our entrance because he came in just behind us. It would take extra time for him to go back to his car from an exit farther down the mall."

"Good thinking," Dad said, nodding his approval. "Anything more?"

"We can find out exactly when Brett left and if anyone was with him," she told Dad.

"When we started to follow to see who Brett was meeting, a woman stopped us." Juli rushed on to describe the woman with the shopping bag. "The officer — we're sure that's who she is — said it was her job. She told us to scram."

Hope filled Dad's gray eyes. "That's the best news I've heard all day. I'll get on it immediately." He raised an eyebrow. "In the meantime . . ."

"We know. Scram. As in leave, get lost, disappear." Juli kissed his cheek and started for the door with Shannon. She turned. "Uh, Dad, does Andrew know the description of the robber matches Brett's?"

"Of course." Dad's keen gaze bored into her, then he soberly said, "Want me to send you two home in a patrol car?"

Shannon gulped and Juli shook her head. "No thanks. We'll take the bus." She paused. "I know you're busy, but if you hear anything, will you please call?"

He tousled her hair. "If I can. Good-bye."

At the bus stop, Shannon giggled. "Talk about here's your cap, what's your hurry," she misquoted. "Your dad practically shoved us out the door."

"Since we don't wear hats, I guess you can say it that way," Juli said, her mind running a dozen different directions. Should she mention the thought that came when she read the postscript on Dave Gilmore's threatening letter? Since the descriptions of the robber and Brett were similar, there seemed to be no reason to keep her suspicions secret.

Dave solved Juli's problem without realizing she had one. He and Ted were waiting for the girls at their home bus stop when they stepped down.

"What are you two doing here?" Shannon asked.

"Thanks for the warm welcome," Ted teased. Sunlight glinted on his brown hair and set sparkles in his blue eyes.

"Did Dad call you?" Juli demanded. "He did, didn't he?" she added when both boys looked too innocent to be believed.

"Okay, okay. He thought you and your mom might like company until he comes home."

Shannon stuck her nose in the air. "Mercy me, 'tis a fine thing that you have to be for bein' told to come see us."

Ted draped an arm over her shoulders and gave her a quick hug. "You know better than that. Why, we'd for bein' camped on your doorsteps if 'tweren't for what the neighbors'd be for thinkin'."

"That's the worst Irish accent I ever

heard," Shannon said in her normal voice, but her blue-gray eyes crinkled at the corners and her clear laugh rang out.

"Now that Ted has put you in your proper place, whatever that is, we'll confess," Dave solemnly said. "We were practically out the door on our way here when Juli's dad called. After hearing the TV news flash, we decided to drop by and hash it over." He ran one hand over his short hair, blond from the summer sun, and lowered his voice. "We'll talk when we get to the house."

Five minutes later, the two boys, Shannon, Juli, and her mother lounged in the shady backyard sipping ice-cold drinks. Mom had also received a call from Dad, and hastily mixed a refreshing punch that blended several fruit flavors.

Dave grinned at Juli. "This is the life." He took another swallow of punch and set his glass down on a nearby table. His blue eyes darkened and he leaned forward. "Jones must be insane to pull a stunt like today's attempted robbery when he's out on bail."

"Shannon and I don't believe Brett is the robber this time," Juli quietly said.

Dave's mouth fell open. "You don't? How come? The TV newscaster said the description exactly matches Brett's."

"It doesn't matter." Juli clutched her

frosty glass. "Unless he's capable of split-second timing, Brett Jones couldn't have been in Mount Vernon when the attempted robbery occurred. He was in the mall talking with Shannon and me just before." In a few short words she repeated the conversation and mentioned the woman with the shopping bag who told them to scram.

Shannon made a face. "I felt like I'd been scolded and told to sit in the corner."

Juli lunged from her chair at the sharp ring of the phone, vanished into the house, and came back wearing a triumphant grin. "Bingo. Dad contacted the officer who was tailing Brett. He didn't meet anyone, just shopped around for a half hour and bought a new shirt." Juli laughed. "I'll bet that sharp-eyed officer even knows what brand and size it is! Anyway, she followed Brett out of the parking lot, but got held up in heavy traffic and lost him. By that time the attempted robbery was already over."

Mom looked puzzled. "Then the incidents aren't related?"

"We don't know that," Dave thoughtfully said. "Remember the robbery at Sean's bank? There were two people that time with similar descriptions." He sat bolt upright and exclaimed, "That's it!"

"What?" Ted inquired.

"Ever since my copy of the threatening note came something's been bothering me." Excitement crisped his voice. "Remember the first part of the postscript? It said IT PAYS TO WATCH OUT FOR YOUR FAMILY. I thought it was a threat to Christy. Maybe there's a hidden meaning." He gave them a significant glance. "Especially when we hear there are matching descriptions. Get it?"

Shannon grew wide-eyed, but Ted's fists shot into the air in a victory sign. "Yes! It could mean Brett didn't write the notes but a relative did." He looked at Dave admiringly. "No wonder Juli took you on as the Gilmore part of Scott and Gilmore, P.I.s. Great deductive reasoning."

Juli didn't have the heart to tell Dave she had already figured out there might be a connection and had discussed it with Dad, Mom, and the Paynes. Why dim her friend's obvious pleasure at coming up with a possible solution by boasting? Instead she casually said, "It makes sense, doesn't it?"

"It sure does." Nothing in Mom's manner indicated she'd ever heard such a theory before. "How about some more punch?"

"Thanks." Dave held out his glass. "I wonder how Brett Jones is feeling right now. He's sure to have heard of the unsuccessful robbery and the shooting. Brett never hurt anyone when he pulled off those bank robberies. He also claimed his gun wasn't loaded. We don't know if he was involved in the robbery at Sean's bank, but I'm glad he isn't involved in this shooting thing."

A few miles away, Brett Jones lay on a rumpled bed in a cheap motel staring at the TV. What was he doing here? Why had he let himself get pulled into this mess? For what seemed the millionth time, scenes from the Mount Vernon robbery flashed on the screen. He watched in horrid fascination as medics carried a stretcher into a hospital emergency room. He hadn't thought anyone would get hurt. That's why he never loaded the weapon he carried.

He shuddered. Thank God he hadn't been in on this afternoon's attempted robbery that went sour! Thank God? Brett laughed bitterly. A little of the stuff he'd heard while trying to determine what those church kids had seen must have rubbed off. A lot of good it would do him. If there really were a God, fat chance He'd have anything to do with Brett Jones. For some weird reason, Kareem Thompson's face came to mind. Brett had really related to him. Kareem knew what it meant not to have a family.

Brett's mouth twisted. So did he. His assorted parents and stepparents hadn't been in a massacre, but as far as he was concerned, the result was the same. None of them cared about him. No one cared except . . .

Brett shuddered again, in spite of the warmth of the room. The robbery this afternoon proved he no longer had even that frail security. Last night he'd learned about the death threats. They weren't like the notes he'd cut from newspapers and sent to frighten Juli Scott and her friends into keeping still about seeing him at the Pizza Palace. These letters were the real thing, born of a fierce loyalty Brett had counted on, but could no longer control.

Following the caravan of vehicles to Birdsview and frightening a little girl were bad enough. Who knew what crazy thing might happen next? If he stayed silent and anything terrible happened to Juli or one of her friends, he'd be responsible. Juli and Shannon's faces swam into his mind. He flinched at the reproach in their expressive eyes, even though he had shrugged it off and swaggered down the mall earlier that day. Maybe if he'd known girls like them years ago, he wouldn't be where he was now.

"If the woman dies . . ." He couldn't finish the sentence.

Hours later, the phone rang. Brett's heart leaped to his throat and parked. "Yeah?" A low mumble answered. He tried to interrupt several times but the monologue went on, broken now and then by wild laughter. Brett felt his blood chill. The caller was so close to being over the edge it scared him. "Don't do anything stupid," he hissed into the receiver. Dead silence followed, then the tinny sound of the dial tone showed the person on the other end of the line had hung up.

Great drops of sweat sprang to Brett's forehead. Things had gone too far. He had to do something, tell someone, no matter what happened to him. "Who, God?" he groaned, not recognizing it as a prayer for help to a God he didn't even know existed. Words from months before came to his feverish brain, words he himself had spoken while role-playing the victim in the story of the Good Samaritan. *"First, I felt scared . . . then angry because people of my own race looked at me and ignored my cries for help. When the Samaritan came, I knew I was history. I couldn't believe it when the guy helped me."*

Then Kareem's voice. *"Which of these three do you think was neighbor to the man who fell into the hands of robbers?"*

Brett got up from the bed, turned off the TV, and stumbled to the door. He stepped out into gray murk. Fog had come in from Bellingham Bay, shrouding the city until the street and stoplights glowed misty. Like a snail with a broken foot, Brett inched his Mustang block after block. He reached his destination, only to find the building dark and quiet. For a moment, he hesitated. Go or stay?

A lifetime later, Brett slid from the bucket seat. In desperation, he walked up the path to the silent building and rang the bell, again and again. A second lifetime passed before a voice called, "Yes? What is it?" The door opened the length of a security chain. "You? At this time of night?" A strong arm grabbed Brett's shoulder and pulled him inside.

The day after the attempted bank robbery in Mount Vernon, Juli received a disturbing phone call from John Foster. His relatives at the Birdsview farm reported hearing strange noises near their house the night before. The local police came out in the morning and looked over the area; everything appeared normal. "It sounds like they're writing it off as unimportant and I just don't feel good about it," John told Juli.

"Pass it on to your dad and the Paynes, okay?"

Juli called Dad at work. "If someone, say a bank robber, wanted to hide, there's no better place to hide than in a place that's already been searched," she grimly told her dad. "It's also not that far from Mount Vernon to the farm. All the guy would have to do is head farther up the mountain until the authorities got through snooping around. It's not like they used dogs to search."

"Thanks, Juli. We'll talk later. I need to contact Andrew and Mary."

Disappointed at not being in the center of things, she had barely hung up when the phone rang again. Nothing mysterious about this call. Kareem Thompson just wanted her father's number at work.

"It's such a letdown," Juli complained to Mom a little later in the kitchen.

"At least the woman who was injured in the attempted robbery is still alive," Mom gently reminded. "We can be thankful for that."

"I know." Shame filled Juli. "It's just that I feel we should be helping more."

"Dad says you're a big help," Mom comforted. "He appreciates your keen mind and the way you see beneath the surface."

"Thanks, Mom. I needed that." She grinned and relaxed, the last time she would do so for hours. A call from Shannon telling them in a high-pitched voice to turn on the TV sent Juli and Mom racing to the living room.

"It has been learned an older couple living on a farm in the Birdsview area has been taken hostage," the newscaster reported. "A man in his late twenties identifying himself as Tod Markham broke into their home a short time ago and ordered Mr. and Mrs. Foster to call the Washington State Police. The police were directed to notify local TV stations, but Markham warns he is armed and will kill anyone who approaches the farmhouse."

Mom's knees gave way. She gave a strangled sound and dropped to a chair.

"No, oh no!" Juli moaned. A blink of the eye later, the message sank in. "Tod Markham is the one who posted bail for Brett Jones, and probably is a relative! I have to call Dad."

"No, Juli." Mom leaped from her chair and caught her daughter before she reached the phone. "Dad has to keep his attention on his job. Your feelings and mine must take second place just now."

Juli stared at her. Everything inside her

longed to hear Dad's voice, to have him tell her the Fosters would not be harmed. That it was all an awful nightmare she'd wake up from and find was fantasy. No. What Mom said was real. They had no right to claim even one second of Gary Scott's attention for themselves when others desperately needed him to carry on.

Thank God for another source of comfort. Juli grabbed Mom's hand, gently pushed her back into a chair, and knelt beside her. "Please, God, be with the Fosters. Don't let them be harmed." No more words would come.

"We place our friends in Your hands," Mom added. "Amen." Then she and Juli began the long, long wait until Dad could come home.

Chapter 14

A few minutes after Gary Scott received Juli's call about the Fosters hearing strange noises the night before, the phone rang again. "Scott. . . . Who? . . . Oh, Kareem." Gary drummed on his desk with a pencil. "Could we make it another time? I'm pretty swamped." The murmur on the other end of the line brought him to his feet. "*What?* Of course. Come in as soon as you can." He cradled the phone and sank back in his chair, his heart pounding. This could be it.

An eternity later Kareem Thompson and a white-faced young man walked into the office. The youth leader looked haggard, but at peace. Strangely enough, so did his companion. "Brett and I talked until four o'clock this morning," Kareem quietly said. "I insisted he sleep before we came to see you."

"Sit down, please." Gary motioned toward the same chairs Juli and Shannon had occupied the previous afternoon. "What do you have to tell me, Brett?" His calm voice effectively hid the feeling of holding a tangled skein of yarn. If Brett Jones furnished a loose end, it could start the unwinding process.

Brett licked his lips, but met Gary Scott's steady gaze. "I have some information, but it will get me in big trouble. Can you help me?"

Gary's heart thumped again. "Before I answer, I need to remind you of your right to have your attorney present. If you waive that right, anything you say can and may be used against you."

"I know. I don't want Sharpe here." Brett sounded positive.

"All right." Gary glanced at Kareem. "I assume you want Kareem to remain."

"Yes. He knows everything I have to say, and a whole lot more." Brett sent a weak smile in the youth leader's direction. "I just hope I can do this."

"Are you aware what plea bargaining is?" Gary asked.

"I think so. Isn't that where a guy agrees to furnish information in order to get partway off the hook for something else he may have done?"

Gary Scott laughed. "That's one way to put it! If that guy also agrees to testify, he can be granted limited immunity. This means he won't be held accountable on those things about which he testifies."

Brett's dark eyes looked anxious. "What if the guy decides to change his plea from not guilty to guilty on lesser charges? Suppose he doesn't want a trial after all. Is — I mean, *would* it be too late if witnesses had already been subpoenaed?"

"Not at all. There would be an out-of-court settlement, which he would sign."

Gary kept his voice even. Brett reminded him of a mouse creeping from a hole an inch at a time, stopping with every move to make sure no cat would gobble it up.

Brett stared at Gary for a long time. The officer never allowed his gaze to waver. Trust must be established before Brett would open up.

"Go ahead, Brett," Kareem urged gently. "You know it's the right way."

"Yeah." He took and held a long breath, then slowly released it. "You better tape this." The corners of his mouth turned down.

Once the tape was running, Brett started. "I did the Chuckanut Community Bank robbery and a couple of others. Tod Markham and I hit the bank where Shannon Riley's dad works."

"Tod Markham would be . . . ?" Dad prompted.

"A cousin. I hadn't seen him for months, didn't know where he was. Somehow he heard about the trial. He came crawling out of the woodwork to put up bail. He has connections. Anyway, I'm the only one he ever cared about and he's the only one who cares anything about me. Tod's been real protective, ever since I was a little kid. He used to beat up the bullies who picked on me."

Brett's face shadowed. "I feel rotten about what I'm doing, but Tod's been acting crazy. He gets that way if he thinks anyone's after me. I just found out he sent those letters. I did the ones before, hoping to keep Juli and her friends quiet, but Tod means business. I told him to lay off, but I'm afraid he won't."

Gary Scott exchanged glances with Kareem, but merely repeated, "Crazy?"

Brett nodded. "It's hard to explain, but when I heard about the Mount Vernon robbery, I couldn't handle it. Getting a few bucks from a bank's a lot different from shooting people. Tod must be losing it!"

"You had a gun when you were on your own," Gary Scott reminded.

Brett stared at his hands. "Like I said before, it wasn't loaded." His face twisted. "Some bank robber. I didn't have the guts to carry a loaded weapon."

"It took a great deal of courage for you to come to my home in the middle of the night," Kareem reminded. He laid a strong dark hand on Brett's arm.

"I guess. It's not easy turning on the only person who ever treated you like something more than dirt. But how can a guy stand by and watch someone get carried into an emergency room just because she was in the wrong place at the wrong time?" Brett wiped sweat from his face. "I keep thinking, what if Tod had shot that little girl out at the farm? Also, what's next? I'm just glad I said *'No way'* to the Mount Vernon thing." He pressed his lips together hard.

Gary steered him back on track. "You said Tod had connections?"

"He was involved in some heavy-duty stuff back east. He was going to get me in, but things got hot. He left me a note saying to head west, then he disappeared. I had enough money to get the Mustang. I picked up a few jobs to keep going."

"If Tod's been big time, why would he risk being arrested for small stuff?"

"Like I said, he's losing it. He also gets a kick out of living on the edge."

"Do you know where Tod is now? Is there anything else you can tell us?"

"No to both questions."

"You have given this information of your own free will?"

"Yes. No one forced me in any way. It was my idea."

Gary Scott hit the OFF button. "Thanks, Brett. You may never know —"

The door burst open. A fellow officer catapulted into the room. "Sorry to interrupt, but a man insists on talking with you. Says it's a matter of life and death. His name is Foster."

Brett Jones turned paper-white. Kareem clenched his hands. Gary hit a button so the incoming call could be heard by the others. "Scott here."

"This is Mr. Foster. My wife and I live on the farm near Birdsview where the church people came for a picnic. A man just broke into our home."

Years of training kept Gary's voice steady. "Yes, Mr. Foster. Go on."

"He says his name is Tod Markham. He's armed and says he will kill anyone who approaches the farmhouse. He wants the local TV stations notified."

"Will Markham speak with me?" Gary demanded.

"I don't know." Gary could picture Foster turning away from the phone. He heard him say, "Officer Scott wants to know if you will speak with him."

An explosive, "No!" sounded in the deathly still room, then the older man said, "I guess you heard that." A definite click showed someone, probably Markham, had broken the connection.

Brett groaned. "I was afraid of something like this."

"We can't take chances," Gary snapped. The same helpless feeling he had experienced a few times in his career when odds appeared insurmountable swept through him. Rage at Markham for terrorizing the Fosters burned it away. Reason returned. He stared at Brett Jones, knowing he faced one of the toughest decisions in his life. The young man in front of him could be his only hope.

God, give me wisdom, Gary silently prayed. He waited. A minute. Two. "Brett, are you willing to risk yourself to save lives? Including your cousin's?"

Brett looked sick. "I-I don't know."

"I'm not asking you to do it for your own sake, although such cooperation is bound to go a long way toward a lighter sentence," Gary told him. "So far, Tod hasn't killed anyone. Taking the Fosters hostage shows he really may be losing it, as you said. It also means you will be required to testify against Tod, but could well make the difference between prison and a death sentence for murder." He stopped, then deliberately said, "It also means you will have to go to the farm and confront Tod. You'll have to talk him into releasing the Fosters and giving himself up."

The inner struggle between always looking out for himself and wanting to do right this time while recognizing possible fatal consequences, showed in Brett's face. Kareem Thompson spoke. "You are at a crossroads, Brett. You can't help the woman Tod shot, but you may be able to save others. You are their only hope. And Tod's. The choice you make right now will affect lives forever. Which is it going to be?"

Brett's gaze shifted from Kareem to Gary. For a moment it appeared he either would not or could not face the situation. Gary shot another silent prayer skyward, this time for the two young men whose background and tragic choices had started them down the wrong paths and made them criminals. "Well?"

Color crept back into the pallid face. The charm and arrogance that had both attracted and repelled Juli weeks before slowly returned. Brett straightened his shoulders and held his dark head high. "What are we waiting for?"

Gary felt like a worn-out dishrag. His hand shot forward and gripped Brett's. Kareem placed his on top. "Thank God! Brett, no matter what happens, you will never regret this day." Without asking permission, he bowed his head and earnestly prayed, "Father, give Brett the words needed to free the Fosters and to prevent Tod from making terrible choices that will destroy him and others."

Unaware of the startling events in Gary Scott's office, Juli and Mom glued themselves to the couch and stared at the TV. Time stumbled by. Sean Riley took off from work early and came to the Scotts in search of Shannon. Dave Gilmore, the Hiltons, Carlos Ramirez, and Molly Bowen arrived soon after.

"John is absolutely wild," Molly reported. "He wants to rush out to Birdsview but his parents won't let him." Her freckles looked splotchier than ever against her pale skin. "It didn't seem right to butt in on the family or tie up the phone, so I told him I'd be here." She broke off. "Look! Something's happening."

Sympathetic looks turned from Molly back to the TV. Juli couldn't believe her eyes. Two Washington State Police cars drove halfway up the lane leading from the main road to the Foster house. Others parked at the end, effectively blocking radio and TV sound trucks. A helicopter hovered above them, obviously under orders not to fly closer. The mountains, woods, and valley looked as peaceful as ever, making it hard to believe a maniac held two people hostage inside. "Markham must have given permission," she mumbled.

"Yeah." Dave hunched closer, so that his shoulder touched hers.

"Shh. The news reporter is saying something." Mom turned up the volume.

"We're live at the Foster farm near Birdsview," the attractive woman said. "In a bizarre turn of events, the man who identified himself as Tod Markham has issued a statement. In exchange for the release of the hostages, Markham is demanding all charges against his cousin Brett Jones, alleged bank robber, be dismissed. He is also demanding immunity against prosecution for taking hostages."

"Can he do that?" Amy quavered.

Her twin brother grunted. "Markham can demand anything he wants. It doesn't mean he will get it." Ted squinted. His voice rose a full octave. "Well, for crying out in the dark, would you look at that?"

Juli stared at the tall young man carrying a

bullhorn who had stepped from the lead police car and started toward the house. She tore her gaze free and focused on the other three men who got out but remained by the car. One wore a familiar uniform. One had flaming red hair. The third . . . she grabbed Dave's muscular arm in a death grip. "Dad? Andrew? Brett Jones? Is that Kareem Thompson?" Her fascinated gaze was fixed on the figures on the screen. "What are they doing? Markham said he'd kill anyone who came near the house!"

"He won't kill Brett, and the others are keeping a safe distance," Mom said. Her shaking voice said she was trying to convince herself. "Tod cared enough to pull this stunt to keep his cousin from being convicted. He won't hurt Brett."

Juli groaned. "I wish we could hear what he's saying."

"You probably wish you were there, too." Dave tried to lighten things up.

"In your dreams! I like sleuthing, but this is far too dangerous for me. I'm perfectly content to let the experts do the arresting. What I don't understand is how and why those four all got there together."

Carlos looked pale beneath his rich tan skin. "I wasn't going to say anything but it doesn't matter now. Someone came to the

Thompsons in the middle of the night. I thought something might be wrong, so I got up. It was Brett Jones. He and Kareem must have talked really late. I think Brett stayed overnight. I had to leave early to be tutored, and when I got home, no one was there."

Brett Jones and Kareem Thompson? Juli glanced at Shannon's excited face. "Brett asked us at the mall to tell Kareem and everyone hi," she said. "Kareem called earlier today to get Dad's office number. Don't you see? It all adds up."

"It sure does," Dave seconded. His blue eyes looked thoughtful. "An incident, maybe the Mount Vernon bank robbery, scared Brett badly enough to know he is in over his head. I'm thankful something he heard when he came to church made him trust Kareem enough to go see him." He looked ashamed. "I wrote Jones off as hopeless a long time ago, but it looks like God didn't."

He never does, Juli thought. She didn't say it out loud. It sounded too preachy. Yet the understanding look that went from face to face showed she wasn't the only one thinking the same thing.

Brett raised the bullhorn and shouted something inaudible. He evidently received a go-ahead, for he continued up the lane, dark hair gleaming in the sun. A second man, strikingly similar in build and coloring, joined Brett on the front lawn. He carried a weapon, but kept it pointed toward the ground.

"What will happen now?" Molly asked. "No one will shoot him, will they?"

"Not at this point. Andrew and Dad must have made a deal with Brett to try and talk Tod out of what he's doing," Juli told her.

"What if he can't?" Amy whispered.

"We'll pray that he does," Mom said softly.

Time had stumbled by earlier. Now it came to a standstill. After a full hour of watching the distant figures talking and waving their hands, the guests reluctantly said they should go. Mom promptly told them she'd order in pizza if they wanted to stay. Phone calls to parents brought permission. No one could bear being away from the TV for long, so they ate pizza in the living room, watching reporters and the camera crews talking among themselves.

"It's getting dark and hard to see," Shannon said some time later. "I hope —"

A flurry of action cut her short. "Something's happening," the newscaster said needlessly. Cameras zoomed in on the two figures on the lawn. "Brett Jones and Tod

Markham are shaking hands." She continued to give a play-by-play account, even though watchers could see what was taking place — despite increasing darkness.

First, Tod handed Brett his weapon, butt first. Chills traveled up and down Juli's backbone. "You don't think it's a trick, do you? A way for them to make a break into the woods under cover of darkness?" Another awful idea came. "What if Tod is just trying to get Brett's fingerprints on the gun to incriminate him in the Mount Vernon shooting?"

"Forget it!" Dave ordered, even though Juli noticed a little pulse start beating in his temple. "No guy does what Markham did for Brett then turns around and involves him in a shooting."

"He might," Juli reminded, so low no one else could hear. "He must know by now that Brett is cooperating with the authorities."

"Don't even think such a thing!" Dave spit out. "Anyway, Brett is unloading Tod's weapon and picking up the bullhorn."

"It looks like it's all over," the reporter announced when Andrew, Dad, and a horde of officers from the other cars met Tod and Brett in the lane and cuffed Tod. He never looked at the cameras, and Brett only said, "No comment" when the reporters asked what he had said to convince his cousin to give up.

"We may never know," Juli told Dave and the others.

Dad said the same thing when he arrived home, exhausted, to face an expectant group of people who had dwindled by now to the Rileys, Mom, and Juli. Mom microwaved him some dinner and they all sat around the dining room table while he ate.

"It doesn't really matter what took place between Brett and Tod, except we all like to have everything tied up in neat little packages," he wearily said. "Life isn't always like that. The important thing is, no one was seriously hurt. We received an update on the Mount Vernon bank teller. It will take time, but she's going to be all right. Tod Markham must answer for a lot of things, but murder won't be part of it."

"We can thank God for that!" Mom rejoiced. "What about Brett?"

"His cooperation tonight will help a lot. He will still have to serve time, but it may work out to his benefit. He will have access to reform programs and the chance to further his education. Kareem wants the church youth group to keep in touch with Brett. Who knows? It might just do some good."

"I hope this doesn't sound selfish," Shannon hesitantly said, "but does it mean Brett won't have a trial?"

"You aren't selfish and, yes, Brett's case will be taken care of with a settlement order. Are you disappointed that you won't be testifying?" Dad teased. Good food and the chance to relax had brought a grin back to his tired face.

Shannon looked solemn. "I'm just disappointed I spent so much time worrying about something that is never going to happen." Relief sparkled in her blue-gray eyes. She put her hands on her hips and said, "I'll bet God was smiling the whole time. Oh, well. He who laughs last, laughs loudest."

For once, Juli didn't correct her. That night in her quiet bedroom with faithful Clue nearby, Juli wrote in her journal:

I am so glad our Thursday trials are over. They've been the pits. Thanks for bringing us through, God. No one else could have worked it out. Now maybe I'll have more time to enjoy the rest of the summer. Time to hike and write. I want to get back to my Christmas story. Time to make what Shannon calls 'the write choice' about entering the newspaper contest. Time to go to

191

church, hang out with my friends, and not receive threatening letters.

Dad told Shannon and me in a mysterious voice that he, Mom, and Sean are planning something "verrry special," starting a week from Friday. Neither of us can figure out what it is. I wonder if Shannon will ever learn to quote things right. Tonight when she said "He who laughs last laughs the loudest," she sounded just like she used to. I didn't bother to tell her she meant "best," not "loudest." Besides, I was the last one laughing and I did laugh the loudest!

Thanks again, God, for listening. And most of all, for always being here for me.

Juli yawned and put down her pen. "It takes a lot of energy to live through roller-coaster days like this one," she mumbled. She lay awake for a few minutes, wondering about Dad's new and wonderful surprise, then laughed and told Clue, "To make a horrible Rileyism, I can *bearly* wait until a week from Friday!" She punched up her pillows and fell asleep.